D0098830

1010 GUARD STREET

The Case of ROE v. WADE

LEONARD A. STEVENS

G. P. PUTNAM'S SONS
NEW YORK

To my grandson,
Samuel Guthrie Neubauer,
age seven days
May 30 1996

G. P. Putnam's Sons, a division of The Putnam & Grosset Group,
200 Madison Avenue, New York, NY 10016.
G. P. Putnam's Sons, Reg. U.S. Pat. & Tm. Off.
Published simultaneously in Canada.
 Printed in the United States of America.
Design by Gunta Alexander. Text set in Garamond.

Library of Congress Cataloging-in-Publication Data
Stevens, Leonard A. The case of Roe v. Wade / Leonard A. Stevens.
p. cm. Includes bibliographical references and index.
Summary: Examines the people, events, and legal questions
connected to the Supreme Court decision that legalized abortion.
1. Roe, Jane, 1947—Trials, litigation, etc.—Juvenile literature.
2. Wade, Henry—Trials, litigation, etc.—Juvenile literature.
3. Trials (Abortion)—Washington (D.C.)—Juvenile literature.
4. Abortion—Law and legislation—United States—Juvenile
literature. [1. Roe, Jane, 1947– —Trials, litigation, etc.
2. Wade, Henry—Trials, litigation, etc. 3. Trials (Abortion)
4. Abortion—Law and legislation.] I. Title. KF228.R59S85 1996
344.73'04192'0269—dc20 [347.30441920269] 96-11286 CIP AC
ISBN 0-399-22812-8 10 9 8 7 6 5 4 3 2 1 First Impression

Contents

Foreword

In 1973 a momentous decision of the Supreme Court of the United States, *Roe v. Wade,* established that a woman's right to personal privacy includes her right to choose whether or not she may have an abortion. The decision written for the Court by Justice Harry Blackmun included an acknowledgment "[of] the sensitive and emotional nature of the abortion controversy, of the vigorous opposing views . . . and of the deep and seemingly absolute convictions that the subject inspires." This was but a mild preview of what the decision would stir up in America.

The abortion issue aroused intense and often angry debate with an intensity lasting longer than any similar issue in the twentieth century. Television viewers saw tens of thousands of citizens marching in Washington for and against *Roe v. Wade.* They also saw crowds of opponents protesting at abortion clinics around the country. The protests even turned to violence that included the tragic murders of clinic doctors and their assistants. The continuing dispute affected the political process from the local to the national level, and it had a serious impact on the workings of the Supreme Court. At the Court what supposedly had been settled came close to being undone several times.

A legal argument often used against *Roe v. Wade* pointed out that a right to privacy is not found in the Constitution or its first ten amendments, the Bill of Rights. This omission, argued the opponents of *Roe,* proved that the "original intent" of those who wrote these great documents did not include privacy as one of the liberties belonging to the people under the Constitution. If it didn't exist, the opponents argued, it obviously couldn't be used to cover a constitutional right to abortion.

This argument did not originate with abortion opponents who came after *Roe v. Wade.* It was also involved in cases decided before *Roe,* and it was argued at great length by the justices deciding the abortion case. In a 1928 Supreme Court case unrelated to abortion, a famous justice, Louis D. Brandeis, provided another definition of the liberty referred to as privacy. He suggested it could be more aptly described as the "right to be let alone," a liberty close to the spirit of the Constitution.

The phrase made sense historically. The founding fathers who drafted the Constitution and its Bill of Rights came from the colonies, which had just won the right to be let alone by the king of England. In framing these great documents, the authors had in mind the words of one of the greatest among them, Thomas Jefferson. Addressing King George III, Jefferson wrote, "They [the colonists] know, and will therefore say, that kings are the servants, not the proprietors of the people." At the time, the liberty of being let alone by government was so self evident it wasn't spelled out in the Constitution, but provisions for such oversights were made in the Bill of Rights' Ninth Amendment, which acknowledged that while specific liberties had been "enumerated" in the Constitution, this should "not be construed to deny or disparage others retained by the people."

So the constitutional right to privacy—or right to be let alone—did not spring out of thin air in 1973 when the highest court in the land relied on it to protect a woman's right to decide whether or not to have an abortion. The struggle of women to retain that right in behalf of birth control and eventually of abortion had been going on for nearly a hundred years before the Supreme Court began to act on their concerns. That history is important to understanding why the Supreme Court came into the struggle and, after considerable turmoil hidden by the Court's traditional secrecy, handed down *Roe v. Wade,* one of the most controversial decisions in its history. The controversy could very well last as long as, if not longer than, the struggle that led up to it.

While the constitutional right to abortion granted by the decision goes on being debated by legal scholars, religious leaders, politicians, the media, and the public in general, this book provides the human story of how *Roe v. Wade* came into being.

Danforth Cardozo III, Esq.
Montpelier, Vermont

1

A Watershed Case

During the afternoon of January 22, 1973, the country's reporters and editors were busy covering one of the most historic decisions made by the Supreme Court of the United States in the twentieth century. It had been announced by the Court around noon. As the media dealt with the complex decision, knowing it would intensify an already overheated national controversy, they were suddenly confronted with a much bigger story: Lyndon Baines Johnson, the only living ex-president of the United States, had suffered a devastating heart attack at his Texas ranch and had died before arrival at the Brooke Army Medical Center in San Antonio. The death of LBJ, the nation's thirty-sixth president, promptly consumed the lion's share of radio and television news time. In the next morning's newspapers the Supreme Court decision, which could have demanded the biggest headlines of the day, was generally allotted comparatively little space with less conspicuous headlines. An exception was the *New York Times* whose front page carried three banner headlines, the top two announcing LBJ's death, and the third stating HIGH COURT RULES ABORTION LEGAL THE FIRST 3 MONTHS. This referred to two articles starting on the left side of page one and continuing inside.

The Supreme Court's seven-to-two decision dramatically changed America's legal stance against abortion (defined as the premature ending of a pregnancy by expulsion of the fetus from a woman's womb). It did so by declaring unconstitutional the laws of forty-six states that prohibited or restricted a woman's right to an abortion in the first "trimester" (three months) of her pregnancy. Actually, two abortion cases were decided that day, but the one chosen by the Court as the "lead" case became the famous one. It was a case from Texas titled *Roe v. Wade.* The other, a Georgia case, was *Doe v. Bolton.*

The Texas petitioner, Jane Roe, was a young woman in Dallas who had been prohibited by a state law from obtaining an abortion to end an unwanted pregnancy. Jane Roe was not her real name but a fictitious one that allowed the woman to remain anonymous. The respondent's name, Henry Wade, was by no means fictitious. He was a well-known Dallas county elected official, a district attorney whose name had been involved with many prominent cases, including his prosecution of Jack Ruby who had shot Lee Harvey Oswald, the alleged assassin of President John F. Kennedy. Wade became the respondent in *Roe v. Wade* because he had been responsible for enforcing the Texas law that had kept Jane Roe from obtaining an abortion. That law, like most of the country's abortion laws at the time, came from the last century, having been first passed in 1854.

While two experienced lawyers, Jay Floyd and Robert Flowers, serving as Wade's attorneys, argued his side of the case before the Supreme Court, a young and inexperienced lawyer,

Sarah Weddington, argued the case as counsel for the anonymous Jane Roe. Weddington's inexperience was one of the most remarkable elements of the amazing story of *Roe v. Wade.* While lawyers appearing before the High Court invariably come with years of experience, she arrived there at age twenty-seven, having finished law school only five years earlier. She had never practiced law in the conventional sense and had made only one other court appearance in a contested case. What's more, she handled Jane Roe's case *pro bono publico* (for the public good without pay). If all this was unusual, so was the fact that the august, all-male justices listened to a female lawyer, which was not a frequent occurrence, and especially to one so young. Abortion laws all across the country were struck down with a single blow, to the amazement of many abortion proponents who had tried for years to change the aged, restrictive statutes with only minor successes. And of course her victory infuriated the multitudes dedicated to preserving the laws that kept abortion illegal. They had already lost their battle in four states—New York, Washington, Hawaii, and Alaska—where abortion had become legal. Now at noon on that chilly January day in 1973, *Roe v. Wade* added the forty-six other states.

Proponents and opponents of legalized abortion quickly prepared statements about the surprise ruling from the High Court. Leading proponents optimistically described the decision as a triumph, marking the end of a long, difficult struggle for the right of women to control their own bodies. Dr. Alan F. Guttmacher, who had worked for years to liberalize restrictive state laws keeping abortion illegal, said the Court's action was a "wise and courageous stroke." Speaking as president of the

Planned Parenthood Federation of America, and referring to the thousands of illegal abortions that had been occurring annually, he explained, "By this act hundreds of thousands of American women every year will be spared the medical risks and emotional horrors of back-street and self-induced abortions. And as a nation we shall be a step further toward assuring the birthright of every child to be welcomed by the parents at the time of the birth."

Such ideas enraged abortion opponents who were seething that January day as they heard of the Court decision. The fury arose immediately from the Roman Catholic Church whose doctrine had been long and firmly opposed to abortion. There were more than fifty million Catholics in America, and their leaders provided the country's most powerful, adamant opposition to legalized abortion. Two eminent cardinals were ready with statements expressing their outrage over what had happened. One, John Cardinal Krol of Philadelphia, spoke as president of the National Conference of Catholic Bishops. The other was Terence Cardinal Cooke of the Archdiocese of New York.

Cardinal Krol said, "The Supreme Court's decision today is an unspeakable tragedy for this nation. It is hard to think of any decision in the two hundred years of our history which has had more disastrous implications for our stability as a civilized society. The ruling drastically diminishes the constitutional guaranty of the right to life and in doing so sets in motion developments which are terrifying to contemplate. . . .

"No court and no legislature in the land can make something evil become something good. Abortion at any stage of pregnancy is evil. This . . . concerns the law of God and the basis of civilized society. One trusts in the decency and good sense of the American people not to let an illogical court decision dictate to them on the subject of morality and human life."

Cardinal Cooke asked, "How many millions of children prior to their birth will never live to see the light of day because of the shocking action of the majority of the United States Supreme Court today?" He then said the seven justices who had voted in favor of the decision had turned the Court into a "super legislature" that had "usurped the powers and responsibilities of the legislatures of the fifty states to protect human life." And the cardinal concluded, "I hope and pray that our citizens will do all in their power to reverse this injustice to the rights of the unborn child."

Reactions from non-Catholic religious leaders were mixed. Widely publicized praise for the decision came from the Reverend Dr. Howard E. Spragg of the United Church of Christ, who seemed to question the political involvement of Catholics in calling on citizens to use their power to reverse the Court action. "The decision is historic," Dr. Spragg said, "not only in terms of women's individual rights, but also in terms of the relationship of church and state. . . . Where religious beliefs vary, American law traditionally establishes the neutrality of the state. The doctrine of one religious group is not imposed . . . on the rest of American society."

But the nation's doctrine of separation of church and state, to which Dr. Spragg referred, was severely tested in the battles fought over *Roe v. Wade* in the next two decades. Those who had struggled so long for legalized abortion and felt that the triumph of *Roe v. Wade* marked the end of their endeavor quickly discovered how wrong they were. The continuing struggle was greater than anything they'd previously experienced. It involved far more people, and it tore at the social and political fabric of America. The opposing forces became known as "prochoice" (for the Court ruling) and "prolife" (against the ruling).

Following their High Court victory, the prochoice advocates quickly began developing competent medical and counseling services nationwide to accommodate women now free to obtain abortions. Recognizing that many doctors and hospitals were unprepared or reluctant to perform abortions, prochoice organizations established a network of clinics designed and staffed to meet the growing demand for abortion services. Their intent was to replace the hazardous, widely used criminal abortion services with safe procedures. They hoped legal, properly performed abortions would soon be widely accepted as a right that women would not easily give up.

But it soon became clear that the newly gained abortion rights could be lost unless the prochoice supporters organized and fought for them. Their adversaries, the prolifers, wasted no time trying to overturn *Roe v. Wade.* So the battle was joined with millions of citizens involved. One side had legions of citizens who sincerely believed, deep in their hearts, that abortion was absolutely wrong. The other side had legions who sincerely believed, deep in their hearts, that *Roe v. Wade* was absolutely right in making abortion a personal choice not subject to government interference. The conflict was aptly pointed up by the title of a book, *Abortion: The Clash of Absolutes,* by Harvard law professor Lawrence H. Tribe.

The clash continued unabated year after year, becoming a

major part of American history in the final quarter of the twentieth century. The fierce antagonisms to *Roe v. Wade* played out in various ways that affected American political and social institutions. For example, the opposition led to:

- unsuccessful attempts to override the Supreme Court's *Roe* decision by amending the Constitution of the United States to give the illegality of abortion constitutional protection;
- many efforts, successful and unsuccessful, to pack the federal courts, from the district level up to the Supreme Court, with judges and justices likely to support antiabortion decisions;
- intense political activities in congressional and presidential elections supporting prolife candidates who would work for the reversal of *Roe v. Wade*;
- campaigning for passage of new state antiabortion laws that could weaken, or even reverse, *Roe v. Wade* if tested by the Supreme Court and allowed to stand; and
- highly visible public demonstrations at abortion clinics to dissuade women from having abortions and staffs from performing them—events that in some cases turned violent, even to the point of murder.

While *Roe v. Wade* qualifies historically as one of many "landmark cases" (those that dramatically affect both the country and the Court itself), a distinguished historian includes *Roe* as one of only four "watershed cases" in the Court's history. In his 1993 book, *A History of the Supreme Court,* Bernard Schwartz defines a "watershed case" by using an analogy drawn by Justice Oliver Wendell Holmes in 1904. The effects of such a case, Holmes said, worked like the pressure of water flowing down a mountain from a watershed, casting doubts on what had previously seemed clear and causing even well-settled principles of law to change. For better or worse, *Roe v. Wade,* won by the young woman from Texas, deserves to be one of the Court's four watershed cases.

What did Sarah Weddington say as counsel for the anonymous Jane Roe that persuaded the Supreme Court of the United States to reach such a historic decision? If one could claim that she did it with a magic word, it would be *privacy*—a word that does not appear in the Constitution. In deciding Jane Roe's case the justices did so by interpreting the Constitution as protecting a personal right to privacy, despite the fact that the Constitution does not mention such a liberty. Their decision rested on a precedent set in a landmark case from Connecticut decided only eight years earlier. In a way, that decision had as much to do with legalizing abortion as did *Roe v. Wade,* although it was not concerned with abortion but with the free use of contraceptive birth-control methods (the intentional prevention of pregnancy by special devices, drugs, etc.). The Connecticut case dealt with a state law passed in 1879, and the two principals who determined what the law did were both historic figures from nineteenth-century America. One whose fame turned to infamy is hardly remembered today. The other, who was far more famous, remains so. The infamous one was Anthony Comstock; the other was Phineas T. Barnum.

2

Two Guardsmen of America's Morals

By 1870 Anthony Comstock, a young man from New Canaan, Connecticut, had become nationally known as a self-appointed, ruthless crusader for the suppression of vice in America. *The Dictionary of American Biography* describes Comstock's crusading as follows: "Utterly incorruptible and tirelessly zealous in the pursuit of what he considered his duty, he spent . . . his years in furious raids upon publishers of obscene and fraudulent literature, quacks, abortionists, gamblers, managers of lotteries, dishonest advertisers, patent-medicine vendors, and 'artists in the nude.' "

Comstock catered to the fears of millions of his countrymen, and his crusade attracted large numbers of followers. This terrified state politicians, and they began passing legislation urged upon them by Comstock. He then took credit for the laws and used them in his crusades. However, the legislation that added most to his fame was adopted by the Congress of the United States and signed by President Ulysses S. Grant in 1873. Officially titled the Act for the Suppression of Trade in and Circulation of Obscene Literature and Articles of Immoral Use, it became widely known as the Comstock Law. As originally drawn up, the measure would have banned only the circulation of obscene literature by the U.S. mails, but in its final form the law had become much broader, making it a federal offense to sell or offer to sell, give away, lend, exhibit or offer to exhibit, publish or offer to publish, or even have in one's possession for any purpose any obscene material. Most important to the future fate of the Comstock Law, it also included language making it unlawful for anyone to use, sell, advertise, etc., any "instrument or other article of an immoral nature, or any drug or medicine, or any article whatever, for the prevention of conception [pregnancy], or for causing unlawful abortion. . . ."

With his law on the books, Comstock received a commission making him a "special agent" of the Post Office Department of the United States. Each year he was provided with a handsome certificate signed by the postmaster general directing that Comstock was to be (1) "obeyed and respected" by everyone connected with the postal service and (2) given free travel by all the contractors carrying the nation's mails. This granted him a right—now unimaginable—to ransack the country's mails in search of obscene materials. Many senders of items that he declared illegal often ended up in prison after the special agent personally arrested and charged them with violations of the Comstock Law.

Having gained this power on the national level, Anthony Comstock offered "his" federal law as a model for state laws that he promoted all over the country. Eventually the law books of forty-six states were directly or indirectly affected, and obscene material, including practically anything that might be used to prevent conception or cause abortion, was illegal.

The immense power acquired and persistently exercised by Comstock for nearly a half century was astonishing. Two years before his death in 1915, he told a reporter for the *New York Evening World*: "In the 41 years I have been here I have convicted persons enough to fill a passenger train of 61 coaches, with 60 coaches containing 60 passengers each and the 61st almost full. I have destroyed 160 tons of obscene literature." He also boasted of having been responsible for 15 suicides among those he had convicted.

Comstock's prodigious efforts made him many enemies. They resented his forcing his brand of morality into the nation's laws, especially in states where he was not a citizen. When Massachusetts passed its version of the Comstock Law, a Boston magazine editor called it a "contemptible conspiracy to deprive people of their liberties." And he asked, "What do the Republican party and Governor Talbot mean by importing this pious scamp . . . to 'regulate' morality in Massachusetts?"

An unusual criticism of the crusading lobbyist came in a letter to the *New York Times* from a Baptist minister. It offered a preview of arguments that would be used against Comstock-inspired laws that were still in force after the middle of the twentieth century. The clergyman wrote, "I protest against the laws and the proceedings of Anthony Comstock, wherein he attempts to regulate and prohibit the sale of certain things hitherto commended by prudent physicians as harmless and yet invaluable to sickly and overburdened mothers." The preacher questioned the invasion of the privacy of homes under Comstock laws, adding that instead there ought to be laws ". . . to discourage the bringing into existence of weaklings; also to guard the mothers from burdens that prevent them from caring for the children they have."

In a typical reply Comstock said, "Evidently this pastor is either crazy, stupidly ignorant, a very bad man at heart, or else he has a very poor way of expressing himself so as to make people understand his meaning."

Such callousness became widely known, and thanks to the great English playwright George Bernard Shaw, Comstock's name became the root of a new, derogatory word in the English language, "Comstockery." It is now found in many dictionaries—one definition being "ruthless suppression of plays, books, etc., alleged to be offensive or dangerous to public morals."

When time came for the provisions of Comstock's federal law to be adopted by his home state, it fell into the hands of Connecticut's far more famous and joyful son, Phineas T. Barnum, who was born in the small town of Bethel in 1810. Although Barnum's main business in the late 1870s was the highly profitable American Museum in New York, he resided in Bridgeport, Connecticut.

Today P. T. Barnum remains widely known as one of America's greatest showmen, if not *the* greatest. His name is still used by the country's largest circus (Ringling Brothers, Barnum and Bailey Combined Shows). But few people realize that Barnum was also a politician, once the mayor of Bridgeport and a representative to the Connecticut General Assembly (state legislature) in Hartford as well.

As a mayor and a lawmaker, the showman's political philosophy was often moralistic—which may have reflected the public mood cultivated by Comstock. The connection, if any, between the two men is not clear; however, the showman was a crusader against the wickedness of humankind—some of which he was charged with himself. For example, when he became mayor of Bridgeport, he promptly ordered the police to close down all the city's houses of prostitution—only to find himself accused of owning such illicit businesses in New York. As a legislator, he certainly opposed engaging in sex outside of marriage, but he was accused of fathering an illegitimate son—a charge some of his biographers concluded was valid.

However, Barnum's main moralistic drive concentrated on the evils of alcohol. Given his oratorical abilities and intense interest in temperance (abstinence from alcoholic beverages), Barnum became the obvious choice for the chairmanship of the General Assembly's Joint Standing Committee on Temperance, which included both senators and representatives. In February 1879 Barnum's committee had referred to it a bill that had nothing to do with alcohol abuse. Titled "An Act . . . Concerning Offenses Against Decency, Morality and Humanity," it clearly reflected the influence of Comstock's federal law and would penalize anyone "who shall manufacture, sell, or advertise for sale any article or instrument of an indecent and immoral nature, or use any drug, medicine, article, or instrument whatever, for the purpose of preventing conception or causing unlawful abortion. . . ."

The measure did not sail through Barnum's committee but encountered a great deal of backing-and-forthing for more than a month. Legislative records do not say why, but the chairman opposed the legislation even though his committee approved it. In the full legislature the Senate voted for the measure, but the House did not and sent it back to the Barnum committee. This time some changes in the bill overcame the chairman's objections, whatever they were. Then, on March

29, 1879, both the House and Senate approved the legislation and the governor signed it into law.

The new Public Act, closely resembling the federal Comstock Law, turned into and remained one of the toughest anticontraceptive laws in the country. In Connecticut it became a felony punishable by fines or imprisonment for anyone—including married couples in their bedrooms—to practice birth control by virtually any other method than abstaining from sex. The law remained on the books for eighty-six years, until 1965.

Fortunately for his memory, P. T. Barnum had too much going for him historically to be seriously demeaned by "Comstockery" and his role in the passage of the harsh statute by his committee. However, the durable old law eventually became subject to a long, fierce battle in his home state, and the results paved the way for *Roe v. Wade.* During the struggle, opponents of the 1879 statute frequently identified it as the "Barnum Law" to emphasize how archaic it had become.

3

The Nurse Who Would Be Heard

Less than six months after passage of the Barnum Law, and at the height of Anthony Comstock's long, repressive campaign, the person who would become his most powerful enemy was born on September 14, 1879, in Corning, New York. The daughter of Anne and Michael Higgins, she would become famous in the next century by her married name, Margaret Sanger. Her renown came from her lifelong fight to free the use of contraception from the tight legal shackles promoted nationwide by Comstock. To a large extent, she was motivated by the horrors of women suffering from abortions that were illegally or self-performed because they were denied the right to control the size of their families by contraceptive means. While Sanger forever despised abortion, her fight for the sexual rights of women led all the way to *Roe v. Wade.*

Margaret Sanger was the sixth child born into a family of eleven children. Growing up in such a large family made a deep impression on her that helped determine the direction her life would take. Her mother, worn down by repeated pregnancies, births, and endless child care, died at age forty-eight, while her father lived to be eighty. The family, neither wealthy nor poverty-stricken, resided on the outskirts of Corning, but Margaret's memory of the city was a key to her future. She never forgot how poor people living near the factories and railroads along the river flowing through Corning had families with many children, while the wealthy people with homes on the hills above the valley had families with few children. Years later she recalled: "Very early in my childhood I associated poverty, toil, unemployment, drunkenness, cruelty, quarreling, fighting, debts, jails with large families [living in the valley]."

Her continuing concern for these conditions contributed to Sanger's choice of a career in nursing. But after she finished her training in New York City and received her credentials as a professional nurse, her marriage to the architect William Sanger interrupted her career. Over the next dozen years she waged a lengthy struggle against tuberculosis and became the mother of three children as well. In the twelfth year of her marriage circumstances finally allowed her to return to nursing, and she began part-time, usually on maternity cases around the city.

Much of what she saw upset her: "Constantly I saw the ill effects of child bearing on women of the poor," she wrote. "Mothers whose physical condition was inadequate to combat disease were made pregnant, through ignorance and love, and died. Children were left motherless, fathers were left hopeless and desperate, often feeling like criminals, blaming themselves for the wife's death—all because these mothers were denied by law knowledge to prevent conception. . . .

"This was so outrageous, so cruel, so useless a law [the Comstock Law] that I could not respect it. I longed to prove its bad effects, to show up its destructive force on women's and children's lives."

That desire grew stronger as Sanger's maternity calls took

her more and more into the nightmare of New York's Lower East Side. During 1912, she realized she couldn't possibly have imagined what she would find in that poverty-ridden part of the city.

"The menace of another pregnancy hung like a sword over the head of every poor woman I came in contact with that year," she recalled. "The question which met me was always the same: 'What can I do to get out of this?' . . . 'It's the rich that know the tricks,' they'd say, 'while we have all the kids.' Then if the women were Roman Catholics, they talked about 'Yankee tricks,' and asked me if I knew what the Protestants did to keep their families down."

Sanger was most appalled by what she saw on Saturday nights in that desperate region of New York. She came upon lines of women, sometimes fifty to a hundred, waiting to get into disreputable offices known to provide inexpensive abortions. When she learned of what happened in the offices, she was furious to think of the risks the women were taking to avoid having more children. The typical abortionist—practicing without medical credentials—offered a quick examination and then inserted a probe into the pregnant woman's uterus, giving it a few turns to disturb the fertilized ovum. The woman was then told to go home and wait for the flow to begin. The flow sometimes continued for as long as four or five weeks, and the victim's loss of blood often led to her being rushed to a hospital for help. Experience had taught her neighbors she would be a lucky woman to return alive.

"I heard over and over again of their desperate efforts [to end their pregnancies]," Sanger remembered, "—drinking various herb-teas, taking drops of turpentine on sugar, steaming over a chamber of boiling coffee or turpentine water, rolling down stairs, and finally inserting slippery elm sticks, or knitting needles or shoe hooks into their uterus. . . . I knew hundreds of these women personally, and knew much of their hopeless, barren, dreary lives. . . . They claimed my thoughts night and day. One by one these women, with their worried, sad, pensive and ageing faces would marshall themselves before me in my dreams. . . . I could not escape from the facts of their misery, neither was I able to see the way out of their problems and their troubles. Like one walking in a sleep I kept on."

Margaret Sanger's ordeal on the Lower East Side finally came to an end with a poor family named Sacks on Grant Street. Sadie Sacks, the twenty-eight-year-old mother of three children, had become pregnant and attempted to abort herself with an instrument borrowed from a friend. She lost consciousness and collapsed on their tenement floor where she was found with her frightened children, ages one to five. The family doctor came and urged that Sadie be rushed to a hospital, but her husband refused permission. Instead a nurse was called for, and Sanger responded.

She spent three weeks nursing Sadie back to health from the brink of death. As Sanger was about to depart, the patient said, "Another baby will finish me, I suppose." The family doctor, who was paying a final visit, agreed and warned, "Any more capers, young woman, and there will be no need to call me."

A few months later Mr. Sacks frantically called for Sanger, and she arrived, along with the family doctor, to find Sadie unconscious. Again she had become pregnant, and this time had gone to a "five-dollar professional abortionist." She was beyond help and died only ten minutes after the nurse and

doctor arrived. Sanger stayed late into the evening, trying to console the frightened children as the distraught father paced the room, moaning, "My God! My God! My God!"

Sanger was so overwrought that she couldn't return to her own family right away. Instead she walked and walked through the city, lugging her heavy nursing bag. Hour after hour, she continued through the dark streets—"dreading to face my own accusing soul"—until three o'clock the next morning.

Arriving home, where everyone was asleep, Margaret Sanger experienced what was clearly the defining moment of her life—and, indeed, a defining moment for the future of American women.

"I entered the house quietly, as was my custom," she was to write, "and looked out of the window down upon the dimly lighted, sleeping city. As I stood at the window and looked out, the miseries and problems of that sleeping city arose before me in a clear vision like a panorama; crowded homes, too many children; babies dying in infancy; mothers overworked; baby nurseries; children neglected and hungry—mothers so nervously wrought they could not give the little things the comfort nor care they needed; mothers half sick most of their lives—'always ailing, never failing'; women made into drudges; children working in cellars; children aged six and seven pushed into the labor market to help earn a living; another baby on the way; still another; yet another; a baby born dead—great relief; an older child dies—sorrow, but nevertheless relief—insurance helps; a mother's death—children scattered into institutions; the father, desperate, drunken; he slinks away to become an outcast in a society which has trapped him."

Sanger remained, transfixed, her mind's eye continuing these mental pictures, until daylight, when, she recalled, "I knew a new day had come for me and a new world as well. . . . I could now see clearly the various social strata of our life; all its mass problems seemed to be centered around uncontrolled breeding. There was only one thing to be done . . . Awaken the womanhood of America to free the motherhood of the world! I released from my almost paralyzed hand the nursing bag which unconsciously I had clutched, threw it across the room, tore the uniform from my body, flung it into a corner and renounced all palliative [offering only temporary, superficial cures] work forever."

She resolved that, Comstock be damned, she would see to it that women would have knowledge of contraception. "I would strike out—I would scream from the housetops," she wrote. "I would tell the world what was going on in the lives of these poor women. I *would* be heard. No matter what it should cost. *I would be heard.*"

With that decision, Sanger claimed, she went to bed and enjoyed the first undisturbed night's sleep she'd had in over a year. When she got up, she told her family she was finished with nursing and would never go on another case—and she kept that promise.

She began her new mission by trying to find information on practical contraceptive methods. After visiting all the major libraries in New York, Boston, and Washington, she concluded they had next to nothing. The Library of Congress, for example, offered only one useless pamphlet dating from the 1830s.

In the autumn of 1913 the Sanger family sailed to Europe, where Comstockery had not hindered the development of contraception. There Sanger found the information she wanted, and in January 1914 she returned to New York ready to write up her findings in a form that even poor, uneducated couples could use to control the size of their families.

Back home she found the militant feminist organizations of the time unwilling to help her. They were fully occupied with women's suffrage, the drive to win women the right to vote. Moreover, the fear of Comstock made them avoid anything even remotely related to contraception. Wait until we have the vote, the leaders kept telling Sanger.

But she felt her cause was much too important to wait. As for Comstock, her strategy was to do what no woman had dared do before: confront the man and his law head-on. Her weapon was a monthly magazine, *The Woman Rebel,* that she single-handedly wrote, published, mailed, and paid for from family savings. The first issue, that of March 1914, opened with an attack on Comstock, then broke his fearsome law by providing information on how contraception could prevent unwanted pregnancies and avoid the horrors of abortion.

When the first issue was mailed, a notice from the post office simply stated "Unmailable." It turned out that half the copies were confiscated, but the other half went through—as did all the April and June issues—but May's was confiscated. Sanger waited for Comstock's legal action against her, but for some reason he held off.

Meanwhile, the response from readers amazed the daring publisher, as letters by the bundle arrived. *The Woman Rebel* also received attention in newspapers and magazines, and it brought Sanger financial assistance and offers from people willing to join her cause and help personally. Soon a nucleus of these supporters formed an organization whose name, the

American Birth Control League, used, for the first time, the term *birth control.*

Besides *The Woman Rebel* Sanger published a pamphlet, *Family Limitation,* which described practical birth-control techniques useful for all women, but especially for poor, uneducated mothers. Sanger had one hundred thousand copies secretly printed in New York and shipped in lots to her supporters at various locations around the United States. They were to address and stamp their copies ready for mailing all at once when Sanger telegraphed a prearranged signal to post them. Her plan was to flood the nation's postal system with the pamphlet before Comstock could stop the flow.

But before this could be carried out, Sanger was finally arrested on an obscenity charge related to her magazine. She and her lawyer, after trying but failing to obtain a delay in her court appearance, concluded the judge would promptly sentence her to jail. While newspaper stories of Margaret Sanger's imprisonment might help her cause, she feared the publicity wouldn't materialize because the papers were so busy covering the outbreak of World War I. Moreover she reasoned that her unpublicized confinement on what might seem like a minor obscenity charge could hurt more than help her cause. The night before the court date Sanger took a train to Montreal, then sailed to England aboard a Canadian ship. Soon she cabled her supporters in America, triggering the simultaneous release of *Family Limitation* by the tens of thousands all across the United States. Waiting to hear of Comstock's reaction, which was slow in coming to war-torn Europe, Sanger remained in exile for several months.

When Comstock learned of the nature and extent of

Sanger's mailing, he was outraged, especially when he couldn't find her. For some time his search was fruitless, but then one day in New York William Sanger answered a knock on his studio door to find a stranger claiming to be one of Margaret's close friends. The man said his wife badly needed a copy of *Family Limitation.* Sanger gave him the single copy he had in the studio. Shortly thereafter another stranger appeared at the door. This one, introducing himself as Anthony Comstock, handed Sanger a warrant for his arrest.

He was tried, found guilty of violating the Comstock Law, and given a choice of a one-hundred-fifty-dollar fine or thirty days in jail. He chose the latter. When Margaret learned of this in England, she booked a nerve-wracking passage across an Atlantic Ocean infested with German submarines and arrived in New York four days before her husband's release from jail. Assuming she was still wanted on the obscenity charge, she turned herself in to the United States district attorney, and the date for her court appearance was set, surprisingly, for three months later.

Obviously the legal climate had changed while Margaret Sanger was away. For one thing, Anthony Comstock was no longer around. At William Sanger's trial he was taken ill, and the illness soon led to his death. Also Margaret Sanger's cause had dramatically gained support during her absence. And not long after her return, the death of her young daughter, Peggy, brought a nationwide outpouring of sympathy for the mother. As the time for her trial approached, the district attorney and the court received thousands of letters and telegrams from all over the country protesting the government's continuance of her case. One of the most publicized letters was addressed to

President Woodrow Wilson from eight distinguished Englishmen, including the writer H. G. Wells. Margaret Sanger's court appearance was twice postponed, and then her case was dismissed.

"Victory and vindication," she wrote. "This dismissal stands as evidence of the power of public opinion and active protest." She then vigorously exercised both of these powers, beginning with a nationwide tour during which she spoke to thousands of people in nineteen cities. The tour produced yards and yards of newspaper clippings and reams of letters—one thousand from St. Louis alone. It also led to the formation of numerous local birth-control leagues.

In the area of "active protest" Sanger, her sister Ethel, who was also a nurse, and Fania Mindell, an ardent supporter who had come from Chicago to help, started the nation's first birth-control clinic. Located in a poor section of Brooklyn, it was deliberately established in violation of the law against contraception. With the three founders wondering how many women would show up, the clinic opened on October 16, 1916.

"Did they come?" Margaret Sanger recalled, "Nothing, not even the ghost of Anthony Comstock, could have stopped them from coming! All day long and far into the evening, in ever-increasing numbers, they came. A hundred women and a score of men sought our help on opening day."

The clinic lasted only nine days but dealt with nearly five hundred cases. On the tenth day the three founders were arrested and taken off in a police paddy wagon. Released on bail, Sanger promptly reopened the clinic—only to be arrested again for operating a "public nuisance." That was the end of the clinic but not the end of the idea, which eventually was widely adopted. She and her sister served short prison terms for breaking the federal and state anticontraception laws. Fania Mindell, found guilty of selling one of Margaret's books on contraception, was fined fifty dollars, but that penalty was reversed on appeal.

Margaret Sanger doggedly continued her crusade for birth control against many odds. Although Anthony Comstock was gone, the opposition to her was carried on by the Roman Catholic Church. She wrote about this, saying, "I remember almost innumerable instances of crude and usually unsuccessful attempts to silence me in those days: hotels boycotted by . . . the Knights of Columbus [an organization of Catholic men] because the managers have provided luncheons to birth-control advocates; halls contracted and paid for, barred at the last minute on account of Catholic Church pressure brought to bear upon their owners; permits to hold meetings withdrawn by mayors or other officials in cities having a powerful Roman Catholic constituency. Priests denounced me in churches and warned those who came to hear me of hell fire and the Devil!"

Subjected to many such incidents, Margaret Sanger continued writing, speaking, and traveling to organize groups nationwide. On one of her shorter trips out of New York she visited Hartford, Connecticut, and though she had no way of knowing it, encountered the beginning of a long struggle that would lead to the *Roe v. Wade* decision a half-century later.

4

The Stubborn Old Barnum Law

On Sunday, February 11, 1923, Margaret Sanger addressed a large birth-control rally at the Parsons Theater in Hartford, Connecticut. It was held in anticipation of a February 13 committee hearing at the state legislature on a bill that would amend the forty-four-year-old Barnum Law to reduce its restrictions against birth control. Sanger explained that she and her followers hoped to eliminate such laws, and free women from the uncontrolled burdens of incessant childbearing. This would allow her to establish hundreds of birth-control clinics where doctors and nurses could help people learn about and use contraceptives.

That Monday Sanger met with several women who were forming a Connecticut affiliate to the American Birth Control League. Two of these women, Katharine (Kit) Hepburn (mother of the famous actress Katharine Hepburn) and a young neighbor, Sallie Pease, were the leaders of the new League, and they remained so into the 1940s.

That Tuesday, in a state capitol hearing room packed with birth-control supporters, Sanger testified before the committee considering the reform bill for the Barnum Law, and she used her time to explain the need for birth control. The main opponents to the legislation were the auxiliary bishop of Hartford and an alderman speaking for Hartford's Catholic Council of Men. Their argument stressed that contraception violated the "natural law" which held that God had provided the sex function for the sole purpose of procreation. Allowed a brief rebuttal, Sanger asked the bishop how the Catholic clergy could say contraception was against the natural law when they themselves prevented conception by practicing celibacy (abstaining from sex). She added, jokingly, that if they really believed in the natural law they could prove it by not shaving their faces and letting their beards grow.

Several weeks later the committee, accepting the strong Catholic point of view, rejected the birth-control measure. This scenario repeated itself over four decades at each biennial (every two years) session of the Connecticut General Assembly. At the same time birth-control advocates in growing numbers lobbied for legislative reform of the Barnum Law, only to be defeated by the Catholic opposition.

Meanwhile some leaders of the Connecticut Birth Control League began pointing out that (1) the 1879 law had never been used and (2) state officials probably never wanted to use it. Sallie Pease and her colleagues decided that, if this were the case, the League might as well try opening birth-control clinics. The idea became reality in the state capital in mid-1935 when the Hartford Maternal Health Center was opened with an impressive board of well-known sponsors. Two women doctors ran the center, which advised married couples on birth-control methods and fitted women with diaphragms (flexible disks inserted in the vagina to prevent conception).

Most surprising, the venture received no newspaper publicity for several months—all to the good, Pease felt. But then the news slipped out when Kit Hepburn inadvertently mentioned the clinic in a speech at Connecticut State College, and the revelation was carried by the Associated Press news wire—and picked up by Connecticut's leading newspapers. A complaint against the clinic was soon received by Hartford's city prosecutor who quietly let it be known he would take no action against Pease and the two clinic physicians unless forced to do so. Meanwhile, editorials in Hartford and New Haven newspapers praised the League's effort, saying the clinic was providing an important medical and social service. The Hartford Maternal Health Center remained in operation, unmolested by the law for five years. Meanwhile Sallie Pease, as president of the Connecticut Birth Control League, opened clinics in eight more cities without encountering trouble from the aged Barnum Law that remained on the books.

Pease and Hepburn had reason to feel their success was part of a nationwide increase of birth-control clinics in the latter half of the 1930s. Over five hundred were in operation by the end of that decade. Furthermore, the introduction of public-opinion polling in those years brought heartening news as pollsters found wide public approval for making birth-control information, supplies, and services easily available. An unexpected revelation of the polls was that respondents favoring birth control included a large percentage of Catholics. The Hartford clinic's records confirmed this, for over 50 percent of the women using the service were Catholic.

More heartening news for Margaret Sanger and her followers came on December 7, 1936, in a decision from a federal court often considered next in importance to the U.S. Supreme Court, namely the United States Court of Appeals for the Second Circuit in New York. The case, with the odd title *United States v. One Package*, involved the federal government's seizure of birth-control devices shipped from Japan to Dr. Hannah M. Stone, the director of Sanger's Birth Control Clinical Research Bureau in New York—and the government lost. When he learned of the decision, Morris Ernst, a well-known attorney associated with Sanger, all but proclaimed the death and burial of the federal Comstock Law of 1873.

Six months later the Sanger forces celebrated another great victory when the American Medical Association (AMA), the leading organization of the nation's doctors, endorsed the distribution and teaching of valid birth-control methods. Sanger declared this to be even more important than the *One Package* decision.

But as these brightening skies cheered birth-control supporters, an ominous thunderhead was forming over Massachusetts. The state also had an unenforced Comstockian law similar to Connecticut's, but on June 3, 1937, it was abruptly invoked as police officers and other officials raided a Salem birth-control clinic, one of seven run by the Birth Control League of Massachusetts. The clinic's records and supplies were confiscated, and three staff members were arrested, charged with violating the state law, and eventually fined one hundred dollars apiece. Clinics in Boston and Brookline were also raided, as was the League's state headquarters where the organization's president and staff members were arrested.

The Salem case was appealed up to the state's highest court, the Massachusetts Supreme Judicial Court, with no success.

Then, in a big and dangerous leap, one more appeal took the case directly to the Supreme Court of the United States. It was a dangerous step because a loss here could set a difficult-to-reverse precedent that could damage future chances to appeal birth-control cases to the High Court. And the fear became real on October 10, 1938, when the Court dismissed the Salem appeal—to the widespread consternation of birth-control advocates. Most upset were Sanger and attorney Ernst. He felt the Massachusetts attorneys had brought a weak, badly stated case that never should have gone to the Supreme Court, and he went to Boston where he accused those responsible of delivering a serious setback to birth control all over the United States.

Coincidentally, only twenty-four hours after the Supreme Court dismissed the Salem appeal, the Connecticut Birth Control League opened its tenth clinic, this one in Waterbury, still assuming the state had no interest in enforcing the Barnum Law. There were significant differences between this clinic, the Waterbury Maternal Health Center, and the first nine clinics. It was housed in a public institution, the city hospital known as the Chase Dispensary, and it was located in the Connecticut city most heavily populated with Roman Catholics. The League soon collided with two young men who were not for letting the old sleeping-dog of a law lie. One was an intensely devoted Catholic priest, Eugene Cryne, president of the Catholic Clergy Association of Waterbury. The other, a lawyer and an ardent Catholic, William B. Fitzgerald, had recently become the state's attorney for Waterbury.

For eight months the Waterbury center quietly went about its business, unnoticed by the press. But then the nature of the new clinic in the Chase Dispensary was revealed by the city newspapers—and Father Cryne read about it. The priest quickly had his association pass a resolution that (1) revealed that a birth-control clinic was operating in the Chase Dispensary; (2) pointed out that Church teachings held birth control to be contrary to natural law and therefore immoral; (3) noted that a state law forbade dissemination of birth-control information; and (4) urged prosecutors to investigate the clinic and if necessary prosecute "to the full extent of the law."

The resolution was adopted on a Saturday and read the following day at the city's Catholic masses. Fitzgerald heard the resolution at the mass he attended, and to him it was as good as an edict from the pope. In short order Fitzgerald obtained a search warrant, went to the clinic, and confiscated its supplies and records. Subsequently he filed criminal charges against the clinic's principal staff: the director, Clara McTernan, and two doctors, William Goodrich and Roger Nelson.

At first Pease, Hepburn, and other leaders of the Connecticut Birth Control League were nervous about the possible effects the Waterbury action might have on the nine other clinics. But on second thought they decided it might be a blessing in disguise by forcing a legal showdown on what they called "the stupid, outmoded law" hanging over their heads for so many years. Now they really had a chance to fight it out in the courts—and that's what they did.

The Waterbury action by the state was fought by the League all the way up to the Connecticut Supreme Court, but the final decision, far from dealing a death blow to the old Comstockian statute, revitalized it, if anything. The League lost, and the court decision delivered a death blow to all its clinics, for Pease and her board hastily decided it would be wise to close the nine remaining clinics. They did so with telegrams on March 20, 1940.

In a final, charitable act toward the three defendants, William Fitzgerald dropped the original charges, stating his belief that the clinic's director and two doctors had not acted with any criminal intent. The defendants were then dismissed by the judge without being sentenced.

Once again Sanger and Ernst were extremely upset by the impact the loss of the Connecticut clinics might have on birth-control efforts elsewhere. Sanger unfairly blamed Sallie Pease and Kit Hepburn for losing the case and demanded that such important legal actions be carefully coordinated with her national staff. But while the loss was disastrous for the Connecticut League, Sanger and her followers could still point to over five hundred birth-control clinics operating elsewhere around the country.

However, Connecticut's birth-control leaders, in less than a year after their legal debacle, went back to court (as opposed to being taken to court) with a test case against the Barnum Law. A prominent New Haven lawyer and recent president of the state bar association, Frederick H. Wiggins, initiated the case at the urging of Wilder Tileston, a sixty-five-year-old Yale Medical School professor and practitioner at the Grace–New Haven Hospital. Tileston had encountered three women whose health or even lives might be seriously threatened by pregnancy. The doctor knew birth control was their salvation, but he couldn't even recommend it without violating the 1879 law. So he pressed for a test case of the law with him as plaintiff and the state as defendant. The three women agreed to participate anonymously as Jane Roe, Mary Roe, and Sarah Hoe.

A year to the day from the Connecticut Supreme Court's clinic-closing decision, attorney Wiggins went to the Superior Court in New Haven and filed a complaint for Tileston against Abraham S. Ullman, the state's attorney in New Haven. The complaint described the three women's serious plight, for which the doctor was legally forbidden to prescribe birth control by the 1879 law that Ullman was sworn to uphold. This, the complaint said, violated Tileston's rights under the Connecticut Constitution and the Constitution of the United States. The Superior Court judge referred the case directly to the Connecticut Supreme Court, where, on June 2, 1942, *Tileston v. Ullman* was decided against the doctor. Again the decision was based on the claim that the court couldn't override the legislature, which had so often chosen not to change or remove the Barnum Law.

This time, the League, which had recently become the Planned Parenthood League of Connecticut, recommended that Morris Ernst decide whether or not to appeal the case to the U.S. Supreme Court. He went for an appeal, which he would handle himself. But then Ernst, who had been so critical of failed legal efforts in Connecticut and Massachusetts, brought a flawed appeal to the High Court which was dismissed on February 1, 1943. The justices in Washington could not agree that Tileston's constitutional rights were violated; however, the Court's majority opinion pointed out that it might have been different had the three patients filed the original complaint instead of the doctor.

This defeat contributed to the discouraging times experienced by the Connecticut birth-control leaders for the remainder of World War II and well into the postwar years. Every two years, their bill against the Barnum Law met defeat at the legislature—even though birth control enjoyed increasing public support and editorial acclaim in leading newspapers. The *Hartford Courant,* for example, said that the 1879 Barnum Law was a "hypocritical anachronism" keeping the state from emerging into the twentieth century.

Connecticut's political reporters certainly knew the reason for the continuing failure. Right after the war, birth control in the state suddenly faced two powerful opponents, both lawyers, both Catholics: John M. Bailey and Joseph P. Cooney. Bailey had become state chairman of the Democratic party, and he ruled the Democratically controlled Senate. His friend Cooney, a former state senator, had become legislative counsel for the Hartford Dioceses (of the Catholic Church), and together they effectively killed all birth-control legislation coming to the Senate.

In 1950, with the leadership of Sallie Pease and Kit Hepburn now in the past, Mary Parker Milmine became president of the Planned Parenthood League of Connecticut. A shadow of its former self, teetering on the edge of bankruptcy, the organization had virtually nothing to show for nearly three decades of struggle. However, Milmine valiantly held it together into the beginning years of the 1950s. With these dismal prospects no one could have imagined the League would become instrumental in winning a U.S. Supreme Court decision that would finally consummate Margaret Sanger's victory over Anthony Comstock—and even more implausible, open the door to a case legalizing abortion in America: *Roe v. Wade.* The chances of all this happening rested purely on luck—which came the way of Mary Milmine in late 1953.

5

A Historic Brief by a Professor of Law

Mary Milmine's first piece of luck turned out to be a next-door neighbor living a few yards from the League's state headquarters in New Haven. In late 1953, Milmine was searching for a qualified executive director willing to start on a meager salary limited by the organization's tight budget. She had no luck, until one day someone pointed out that a woman living nearby had recently been an executive director and was looking for a job. It turned out that the neighbor, Estelle Trebert Griswold, had the desired qualifications but knew nothing about birth control. She admitted she had never even seen a diaphragm—and couldn't imagine what she could do for the League. Milmine explained that the League was virtually down-and-out, and it offered a real challenge for someone able to take over and again make something of the organization. The idea of the challenge appealed to Griswold, and that, with her need for work, led her to say yes. She went to work on January 1, 1954.

The new executive director learned fast and built up the League's membership and finances. By 1956 she had developed an active service referring Connecticut women to cooperating birth-control clinics in nearby Westchester County,

New York, and in Providence, Rhode Island. Meanwhile, Griswold concluded that legislative reform of the 1879 law was impossible and the only solution would be a case taking the League back to the nation's highest court.

In 1958 a prospect for such a case showed up: Charles Lee Buxton, chairman of Yale's Obstetrics and Gynecology Department as well as a practicing doctor at the Grace–New Haven Hospital. Like Wilder Tileston before him, Buxton had a number of patients whose health could be seriously jeopardized by pregnancies that might be avoided if it weren't for Connecticut's Barnum Law. Now, fourteen years after the defeat in *Tileston v. Ullman,* Buxton wanted to try again, but this time with the patients as well as the doctor filing a complaint against the state.

And now there came a second piece of luck for Mary Milmine's League. One day a professor at the Yale Law School, Fowler Harper, met a former student who was about to be married. The young man mentioned how exasperated his bride-to-be had become over the state law against birth control. Since the couple were not prepared to have children right away, she contacted the Planned Parenthood League to learn about birth control, but the staff could only refer her to a Portchester, New York, clinic. Using up most of a day, she drove there, learned what she needed, was fitted with a diaphragm, and returned home. She found it almost impossible to believe that in her day and age a state would keep such a law on its books.

Something about this story infuriated Fowler Harper. While he knew a lot about the birth-control cause, he had not acted as a lawyer in its behalf. But now the young couple's experience made Harper decide to do something about the old law.

He soon met with Lee Buxton, learned of his patients' potential cases, and agreed to try taking them to the U.S. Supreme Court. Harper also contacted Catherine G. Roraback, a young practicing attorney who had graduated from the Yale Law School. He asked her to take Buxton's cases up through the Connecticut courts. Then, assuming they would lose all the way, he asked if she would help him appeal the decisions to the High Court in Washington. Roraback agreed and began by filing complaints for five cases against Abraham S. Ullman, the New Haven County state's attorney. The five included the doctor's case (*Buxton v. Ullman*), and four others from patients which were lumped together under the title of one of the cases, *Poe v. Ullman* (that of a couple using the anonymous names Paul and Pauline Poe).

The complaints, which claimed that the 1879 law conflicted with the appellants' constitutional rights, lost in the New Haven court and were then appealed to the Connecticut Supreme Court. Here the appeals were unanimously denied; the constitutional issues were ignored, while the court claimed it had to respect the continuing legislative support for the Barnum Law.

Fowler Harper promptly began preparing appeals to the U.S. Supreme Court with a "jurisdictional statement" explaining why the Court should accept the cases. Then, if accepted, the lawyers on both sides would be invited to file written briefs arguing the cases for the petitioners (Buxton and his patients) and for the respondent (the state of Connecticut). Next the justices, on a set date, would hear "oral arguments" from the attorneys, then meet in private and decide how they would vote.

In his written submissions to the Court, Harper made legal history by arguing that the Barnum Law violated a personal liberty of Buxton's patients protected by the nation's Constitution. He wrote knowing that the word describing that liberty, *privacy,* was not in the text of the Constitution. He pointed out, however, that the High Court had previously made decisions recognizing that certain forms of personal privacy were protected by the Constitution. Over thirty years earlier, two such cases said that parental decisions about the upbringing and education of children were to be treated by government as private. Then in 1928, in a dissenting opinion, one of the Court's most famous justices, Louis Brandeis, described the right to privacy as the "right to be let alone—one of the most comprehensive rights and the right most valued by civilized men." And in 1942 the Court struck down an Oklahoma law providing for sterilization of certain sex offenders—and, in so doing, established that the right to reproduce was one of the basic civil rights of people that should be let alone by the government.

These precedents helped Harper frame what he wrote, declaring that his appeal was bringing another form of privacy to join those already recognized as being protected by the Constitution. Now he proposed that the Connecticut statute violated the most private part of the petitioners' homes, which he pointed up, saying, "They want to be let alone in the bedroom." Harper repeatedly emphasized that the old law, supposedly enacted to promote public morality, now "mercilessly" invaded the plaintiffs' privacy. "When the long arm of the law," he said, "reaches into the bedroom and regulates the most sacred relations between man and wife, it is going too far."

On the first and second of March 1960, the Supreme Court

heard oral arguments on *Poe et al. and Buxton v. Ullman,* then the justices took over three and a half months to hand down a decision. Five of the nine justices voted to dismiss the case, with the Court's majority opinion written by Felix Frankfurter, the renowned justice appointed in 1939 by President Franklin D. Roosevelt. Frankfurter said that the Court's great judicial power should be used to strike down a state law only in behalf of a citizen "who is himself immediately harmed, or immediately threatened with harm, by the challenged [law]." Noting that since the plaintiffs had no "realistic fear of prosecution" under the Connecticut law, the Court had been asked to umpire "debates concerning harmless, empty shadows"—which it could not do.

Justice William Brennan, one of the five voting for the dismissal of *Poe,* filed a concurring opinion agreeing that the case posed more of a theoretical discussion than a real-life situation wherein the petitioners faced a dilemma caused by the state's enforcing the law. But in his opinion Brennan provided a tip as to the kind of case that would probably receive the Court's approval. He said that if another controversy should "flare up" over the opening of birth-control clinics, it might provide what was needed in this case for the Court to address the constitutional issue involved.

An important dissenting opinion was filed by Justice John Marshall Harlan, one of the four favoring *Poe,* and the dissent had much to offer for the future of the privacy issue from Connecticut. Harlan called the Barnum Law an "obnoxiously intrusive" statute making it a criminal offense for married couples to use contraceptives. And he labeled it "an intolerable and unjustifiable invasion of privacy in the conduct of the most intimate concerns of an individual's private life."

Coincidentally, on the same day that *Poe* was dismissed, the Supreme Court handed down a landmark decision, *Mapp v. Ohio,* involving the Fourth Amendment to the Constitution. The Fourth protects the most elementary form of privacy, that of a person's home, in which officials are not to conduct unreasonable searches and seizures without a legally obtained warrant issued for good cause. This right to privacy, which had been widely abused in most states, was substantially restored by the *Mapp* decision.

The *Poe* dismissal did not surprise Estelle Griswold. In fact, she had been preparing for it by planning and obtaining her board's approval for the very kind of "flare up" mentioned in Justice Brennan's opinion. She immediately looked for a rental property where she and Lee Buxton could open a New Haven birth-control clinic in violation of the Barnum Law. If the clinic was not closed down by the state, her plan called for opening others, one after another, in other cities until one was closed by the police.

A New Haven clinic was opened on November 2, 1961, over twenty years after Sallie Pease had been forced to shut down the last such clinic. In an approach unlike the quiet clinic openings of the past, Griswold held a well-attended press conference making it clear that she and Buxton were flouting the law. As the news spread across Connecticut, she hoped someone reading it would bring the law down upon the violators' heads.

That soon happened, thanks to a most unlikely individual, the night manager of a nearby Avis rental office. He was James Marris, a Catholic and father of five children. The news of the clinic opening outraged Marris. He felt such a place was comparable to a house of prostitution and should never be allowed in New Haven. When nothing officially was done about it, Marris began a personal campaign—visiting, telephoning, and writing to every official from the state police to the governor of Connecticut—demanding that the clinic be closed and the perpetrators arrested.

It took Marris little more than a week to stir up a local prosecutor who sent two policemen to the clinic where they were amazed to find the director, Estelle Griswold, delighted to see them. She went out of her way to provide everything the officers needed to prove the Barnum Law was being violated, including the names of some patients who had declared their willingness to serve as witnesses. James Marris, whether he knew it or not, had become the clinic's best friend, saving the Planned Parenthood League a lot of time and money by not having to open clinic after clinic to bring about what he had accomplished in a week or so.

Following their arrests, Griswold and Buxton were soon defendants in the case of *State of Connecticut v. Estelle T. Griswold and C. Lee Buxton.* With Catherine Roraback representing them in the state courts, they went to trial and were convicted before a judge without a jury on January 2, 1962. The hasty trial was uneventful except for the removal of James Marris from the courtroom after he stood up on his seat among the spectators and attempted to address the judge.

The Avis manager's success was not repeatable as the case went up through the state court system. It took over two years to obtain a decision from the Connecticut Supreme Court upholding the conviction of Griswold and Buxton—all according to Estelle Griswold's plan.

With Catherine Roraback's assistance, Fowler Harper immediately began preparing an appeal to the Supreme Court of the United States. Now the defendants became the appellants under the condensed title *Griswold v. Connecticut.* This time Harper worked with a greater sense of what might convince the justices that the Barnum Law threatened the constitutionally protected rights of Connecticut citizens. For guidance the Yale professor had the High Court's opinions from the *Poe* decision. Also, the constitutional questions involved had been recently and helpfully discussed in law journals and other publications. And Harper had the help of persons from sympathetic organizations, like the American Civil Liberties Union, the national Planned Parenthood organization, and even a Catholic group, the Catholic Council on Civil Liberties.

Harper's main thrust in his submissions to the High Court maintained that Griswold and Buxton had been convicted in violation of a right to privacy protected by the U.S. Constitution—and in making the case he especially relied on the Constitution's Ninth Amendment (one of the Bill of Rights). He used it to deal with the fact that the right to privacy was not a personal liberty cited in the text of the Constitution. He argued that the means for including privacy as such a liberty was provided by the twenty-one words of the Ninth Amendment: *"The enumeration in the Constitution of certain rights, shall not be construed to deny or disparage others retained by the people."* Harper took this sentence as saying the Constitution's framers (authors) recognized the document could not be expected to "enumerate" all the liberties that might rightfully belong to future citizens. The lawyer then proposed that he was bringing such an "unenumerated" liberty for approval by the High Court. He referred to the liberty as "the sanctity and privacy" of spouses in their marital relations, and he claimed this was "precisely the kind of right which the Ninth Amendment was intended to serve." And finally he argued that because Connecticut's 1879 statute denied this right to citizens, it should be declared unconstitutional by the Court, thereby reversing Griswold's and Buxton's conviction.

On December 7, 1964, the Supreme Court accepted the *Griswold* appeal, but by this time the man who had barely lost *Poe* and hoped to redeem the loss with *Griswold* was too ill to continue. Fowler Harper had just entered the Grace–New Haven Hospital at the end of a losing battle against prostate cancer. Knowing that his days were numbered, he called on a Yale colleague and old friend, Tom Emerson, to take over the case. Harper died on January 8, 1965, as Emerson was hard at work on the case, writing the briefs his friend would have submitted, then preparing for oral arguments which the Court held at the end of March.

When the numerous briefs were filed and the arguments heard, the justices had before them a thicket of issues involving several amendments to the Constitution, but most of the nine men sensed that *Griswold v. Connecticut* would lead to a landmark decision with important future ramifications. Their private conferences soon revealed that a solid majority existed for reversing the Griswold-Buxton conviction. When a tally was made to see how each justice intended to vote, it came out seven to two in favor of reversal.

Chief Justice Earl Warren assigned Justice William O. Douglas the job of drafting an opinion that a majority of the Court (five or more justices) could join. He worked and reworked the opinion until finally he had a bare majority agreeing with it, and it became the Court's majority opinion. In total, *Griswold v. Connecticut* was handed down with six different opinions. They included Douglas's majority opinion, three concurring in the decision but not joining the majority opinion, and two dissenting opinions from the justices voting against the decision, Hugo Black and Potter Stewart.

The variety of opinions favoring *Griswold*—while agreeing that the right to privacy in marital relations was the central constitutional issue—reflected confusion as to where in the Constitution the right came from. Various viewpoints saw it coming in different ways from one or more amendments to the Constitution. One of those ways suggested by Justice Douglas advanced the vague assertion that specific guarantees of the Bill of Rights (the first ten amendments) have "penumbras" (a penumbra means a periphery or fringe around something) that create zones of privacy. As if he were asking his brethren simply to give it some thought, Douglas quoted the Ninth Amendment without explaining why. He finally summed up by saying, "We deal here with a right of privacy older than the Bill of Rights."

Justice Black, who had become one of the Court's great liberals, filed a stern dissent—twenty pages that he later described as "the most difficult I have ever had to write." He found the old Barnum Law "abhorrent, just viciously evil, but not unconstitutional." However, he was deeply worried about how the majority of the Court concluded that the Constitution protected "a broad, abstract and ambiguous concept" of privacy. He feared that what was happening might encourage the approval of other concepts simply not found in the Constitution. This was no way to change the great document, he argued; that could only be done by amending it (with the approval of three fourths of the states). He was appalled by the use of the word *penumbra* by his longtime friend Justice Douglas, and later Justice Black asked rhetorically, "How could Bill come up with that?"

Nevertheless, observers and historians of the Court recognized that *Griswold v. Connecticut,* which was announced on June 7, 1965, gave birth to a constitutional right to privacy, while reversing the conviction of Estelle Griswold and Lee Buxton by holding that Phineas T. Barnum's resilient old law was unconstitutional.

Across the country, voices deplored what they felt was an unsupportable revising of the Constitution, as did Justice Black in his dissent, and the outcries would be heard far into the future. But many more voices celebrated *Griswold v. Connecticut.* They included its namesake, Estelle Griswold in New Haven, and an eighty-five-year-old woman in Tucson, Arizona, Margaret Sanger, who knew her battle against the legacy of Anthony Comstock had finally been won.

Margaret Sanger died fifteen months later, assured that her remarkable efforts in behalf of birth control were safe from the kind of laws that had tried to stop her. But she did not know that the basic right to privacy behind this victory would soon be found at the core of another, far more amazing Court decision, legalizing a form of birth control she abhorred: abortion.

6

The Political Power of Thalidomide

Estelle Griswold, Lee Buxton, and all who followed Margaret Sanger's lead concentrated on birth control by contraception and not by abortion. However, three years before the U.S. Supreme Court decided *Griswold v. Connecticut,* a continuing news story from Arizona prompted a great many Americans to think seriously for the first time about birth control by abortion.

In 1962 Sherri Finkbine, the twenty-nine-year-old mother of four young children, was well known for her popular children's program on a Phoenix television station. That summer, Finkbine found she was pregnant for the fifth time. She was happy about it; but given the pressures of her family and television program, she needed to relax, so she took a tranquilizer that had been in a medicine cabinet, unused, since her husband, Robert, had brought it from England a year earlier. She then happened to read a newspaper article about thousands of deformed babies born in Europe, Australia, and Canada to mothers who, during early pregnancy, had used a tranquilizer called thalidomide. Suddenly worried that the pills from England might affect her pregnancy, she asked her doctor to check them out. To her horror, he found they contained thalidomide. Her distress increased when the doctor showed her pictures in a recent medical journal of grotesquely deformed "thalidomide babies" who, instead of arms and legs, had flippers like those on seals.

The doctor immediately recommended that he perform a "therapeutic abortion" at the local Good Samaritan Hospital, so that Finkbine would avoid what thousands of mothers and their deformed babies were suffering elsewhere. The doctor explained that, strictly speaking, abortion was illegal in Arizona, with one exception: to save a mother's life. He added that the limitation was routinely overlooked in situations comparable to the Finkbines'. Taking care to say that the birth could seriously affect her mental health, Sherri Finkbine could easily obtain permission for the abortion from a three-doctor committee at the hospital. The committee routinely granted permission in such cases. With the approval, the abortion could be performed at the hospital—well within the pregnancy's first three months, the allowable period of time for the surgery.

The Finkbines, who would ordinarily never have considered an abortion, agreed to have one. Sherri Finkbine then kept an appointment with the hospital committee, bringing statements from two psychiatrists confirming that the birth of a thalidomide baby could seriously affect her mental health, even to the point of driving her to suicide. The three-doctor committee indicated their approval, saying that after a routine agreement by the county medical association, Finkbine's doctor could perform the abortion at the hospital.

But suddenly all the routineness ended after Sherri Finkbine innocently revealed her plight in a conversation with the wife of a local newspaper editor. The Finkbine case was soon all over the media, in Arizona and across the country. The county medical association immediately delayed approval until its lawyers could review the case. The Finkbines' doctor knew the abortion was in trouble, for approval now depended on a legal, rather than a medical decision.

He was right. The Finkbines became desperate, retained a lawyer, and sued the county, hoping to force approval for the abortion, but this only prolonged the delay. Everyone involved sympathized with the couple but blamed unavoidable legalities for holding up the abortion. As the three-month deadline approached, the Finkbines decided the only way to terminate the pregnancy was to go to a country where abortions were legal. Their choices narrowed down to Japan or Sweden. They first decided on Japan, but a visa problem made them change to Sweden. With no time to waste, the couple hurriedly caught a flight to Stockholm with no more than the assurance of a Swedish newspaper correspondent that an abortion could be arranged there. In Sweden, however, they encountered another nerve-wracking delay while the Swedish Royal Medical Board agreed the abortion could be performed. Finally, in the thirteenth week of Sherri Finkbine's pregnancy, on the very borderline of when it was considered safe, the abortion was performed at the Karolinska Hospital. Reporters waiting for the results were told by doctors that, yes, the fetus was badly deformed.

Those reporters and scores of others who had followed the Finkbines in the summer of 1962 left Sherri Finkbine, the relatively unknown TV host of a children's program, with international fame she didn't enjoy. That she had widespread sympathy was confirmed by a Gallup poll, which revealed that 52 percent of the respondents approved of what she had done, 32 percent disapproved, and 16 percent had no opinion.

From among the disapprovers came some of the most painful experiences of the Finkbines' time in the limelight. Their mail included many hostile letters denouncing their decision—including one letter that outraged Sherri Finkbine with an offer to adopt the deformed baby if she would allow it to be born. Some of the most disturbing opposition to the abortion came over the Vatican Radio in Rome, heard in Sweden. The voice of the Roman Catholic Church accused the Finkbines of committing murder, because the aborted fetus, from conception, had been a human being.

Sherri Finkbine had never been an advocate of a woman's right to decide for herself whether or not to have an abortion, nor would she become a prochoice advocate after her agonizing effort to terminate a pregnancy accidentally affected by her having taken thalidomide. However, her widely publicized case turned out to be a powerful force for abortion reform in the United States.

The story of the mother from Phoenix revealed to millions that the country's abortion laws had become a hypocritical mess. They had been developed for good cause and administered by the medical profession to confine abortions to legally approved methods provided by licensed physicians for "therapeutic" purposes, like saving a mother's life. But, as dramatically demonstrated by the Finkbines' case, the laws were being routinely and quietly circumvented, leaving the choice of who should or should not have abortions up to doctors and hospitals.

The Finkbines' story certainly had an influence on the future of abortion in America. The couple's dilemma caused thousands of people, and especially feminist leaders, to talk openly for the first time about a previously taboo subject and to discuss the legal and social issues involved. People also found, as the Finkbines did, that opening up the subject uncovered sharp divisions with little middle ground for agreement.

Abortion in America was not always the forbidden, divisive subject it had become in the twentieth century. In 1789, as the new nation's Constitution took effect, none of the thirteen original states outlawed abortion, nor would any state do so during the next thirty-two years. Meanwhile, common law (that made by English judges over the centuries and relied upon in early America) permitted abortion up to the time in pregnancy called "quickening," when a woman could perceive the first movement of a fetus. Until medical science revealed the true nature of a pregnancy, quickening remained the one dependable sign among others that told a doctor a woman was definitely pregnant. In those years quickening was the key to many decisions involved with human birth. For example, it was long considered to reveal the beginning of human life; therefore, common law did not equate abortion with murder in the months before quickening, but did so after quickening.

The first state law against abortion was passed by Connecticut in 1821. It was designed to outlaw abortion carried out only after quickening and then only by the extremely dangerous method of having the mother ingest just enough of a lethal poison to kill the fetus but not herself. As the Connecticut law indicated, the medical profession was becoming concerned about the increasing, widely advertised trade of unprofessional, unregulated abortionists, as well as their various home remedies and techniques for self-induced abortions. To be rid of them involved a long struggle, for they were still at work far into the twentieth century. Nevertheless, the medical profession succeeded with extensive lobbying campaigns in the 1800s, and abortion eventually became a criminal offense in every state of the union. Many of the laws included an exception for therapeutic abortions, usually to save a mother's life.

All during the two-hundred-plus years of the nation's history abortions occurred in surprising numbers. Legally or illegally, women found ways of terminating pregnancies. All too many of the methods put women's health and lives at risk. The annual rate of abortions was often influenced by social changes. It was less prevalent in early rural America because of the need for large families to provide labor on family farms. When the country became urbanized with industrial cities fostering large pockets of poverty, abortions increased as women tried to keep down the size of their families. This was also evident during the Great Depression of the 1930s when the armies of unemployed could not afford large families.

As time passed, the therapeutic exceptions to the abortion laws were more liberally construed, not by lawmakers, but by doctors, case by case. During the Depression, for example, poverty sometimes served as a reason for making such exceptions. After World War II psychiatric problems were included as reason for therapeutic abortions. The numbers of such abortions eventually dropped as medical review boards came into the decision making. Even so—as the Finkbine case illustrated—doctors and review boards still allowed the surgery knowing they were violating the law. By the 1960s overlooking abortion laws without changing them showed up in statistics indicating that over a million technically illegal abortions a year occurred in the United States. This did not include abortions performed on American citizens in foreign countries. Nor did the statistics tell that many abortions were badly performed—as demonstrated by an "infected obstetrics" ward in a Los Angeles hospital where over fifty beds were kept ready for botched abortions. What's more, crime statistics in those days showed that illegal abortions were hardly ever prosecuted.

The increase in laws being broken without prosecutions, virtually making abortion available when a doctor wanted it, clearly called for change, and the need began to be addressed remarkably fast in the 1960s. Help for legislators favoring such changes was offered in 1959 by the American Law Institute in a revision of its Model Penal Code. A few years later legislative attention to the Institute's suggestions received a shove from public reaction to the Finkbine case and also from an outbreak of German measles, which caused deformed babies to be born to some mothers stricken during pregnancy. Meanwhile increasing public discussion of abortion questions led to a virtual groundswell of public attention to the problem. Articles about abortion appeared in newspapers, national magazines, and medical and law journals. In 1965 the CBS television network presented a documentary titled "Abortion and the Law," and that year the *New York Times* carried a groundbreaking editorial calling for reform of abortion laws.

Meanwhile, existing and newly formed organizations began pressing for reform of the laws. In 1967 the one-year-old National Organization for Women (NOW) held a vigorous debate on abortion at its national meeting, followed by the addition of the "Right of Women to Control Their Reproductive Lives" to its "Women's Bill of Rights." That year the political pressure for reform began to produce results as twenty-eight state legislatures took up reform measures providing more reasons for allowing abortions. Colorado and California passed such laws. In the latter, Governor Ronald Reagan, who would go to the White House as a strong opponent of abortion, reluctantly signed the bill liberalizing the Golden State's abortion law. By 1970 a total of twelve states had adopted reforms, and seven more would do so in the next three years.

However, the anticipated increase in abortions failed to materialize, especially in California and Colorado. It became clear that liberalized laws were hamstrung by bureaucratic requirements that kept many women from having abortions, especially poor women. Nevertheless many of the advocates of reform felt it could succeed with patient, continued pressure on state lawmakers. But not all the activists agreed, and some felt they had remained quiet for too long about what they saw as the medical profession's far too "timid" approach to the problem. Out of this came the belief that the only answer was an all-out campaign, not to reform, but to repeal criminal abortion laws.

This approach quickly gained surprising support. In 1968 a vote by Planned Parenthood's members called for the abolition of all antiabortion laws, and in 1969 the National Association for the Repeal of Abortion Laws was formed "to secure and preserve the right to safe, legal abortion for all women." Meanwhile the repeal movement received endorsements from a number of well-regarded Protestant clergymen in some of the country's major denominations. Surprisingly, twenty-one

New York clergymen formed a Clergy Consultation Service on Abortion, using an 800 number to provide abortion referral information to any woman requesting it. And especially important, some of the medical profession's strongest advocates of reform switched to supporting the repeal of abortion laws.

The success of the repeal movement generated enough political power to persuade many state legislatures to consider legalizing abortion, and in 1970 Hawaii became the first state in the nation to repeal its criminal abortion law. Right away New York State, following an all-out battle between feminists for repeal and the Roman Catholic Church against, voted on a repeal law. The measure passed the Senate but was expected to lose in the Assembly (house of representatives) by a close vote. But then it won by a single vote resulting from a last-minute switch from no to yes by Assemblyman George M. Michaels. Despite the opposition of his heavily Catholic constituents to repeal, Michaels, recognizing during the roll call that his no vote was killing a law his family favored very much, deferred to them rather than the voters. He assumed it would end his political career—and it did.

Then in 1970 Alaska's governor vetoed a repeal bill, but the legislature had enough votes to override the veto, thereby legalizing abortion in the "Land of the Midnight Sun." And in the same year the Washington state legislature left the abortion question up to a public referendum to be held on election day. This worried national repeal advocates who feared that voters would reject their cause and damage it all over the country. But the fears were unfounded, for 56 percent of Washington's voters in the November election approved repeal.

While 1970 seemed like just the beginning of states legalizing abortion, it really marked the end, for the opponents increased in numbers and political power. The Roman Catholic Church became more vigilant and cultivated allies who also opposed the abolition of criminal abortion statutes. The early stages of what would become the prolife movement became evident, and state legislators reacted to them.

A Cincinnati doctor, John C. Willke, and his wife became the most active of the increasingly numerous abortion opponents. Their "Handbook on Abortion," illustrated with startling photographs of aborted fetuses, provided the emotional rhetoric and techniques that antiabortion forces would use for many years. And the Willkes' glossy, full-color handout, "Life and Death," nicknamed the "fetus brochure," was printed by the hundreds of thousands for use by antiabortion campaigners. The couple's effectiveness as political organizers was proven in 1972 in Michigan and North Dakota where referenda were held on the repeal of abortion laws. Early opinion polls predicted the repeals could win in both states, but the Willkes and their literature reversed what the polls had predicted, and voters rejected both repeal efforts—by 62 percent in Michigan and 77 percent in North Dakota.

The serious defeats turned the early 1970s into depressing times for the repeal movement, while those opposing repeal were encouraged. At this point it would have been hard to believe that one of the more durable of the nation's abortion laws was about to become involved in the most dramatic, unexpected event in the history of abortion in the United States.

That law, which was passed by Texas in 1854, made it a crime to perform an abortion or to provide a woman with the means to cause an abortion in that state. The penalty for violating the statute was five years in prison if the woman had consented to the abortion, or ten years if the surgery had been performed without her consent. The statute allowed that the death penalty could apply if a woman died from an abortion or attempted abortion. The law's one exception allowed for an abortion recommended by a doctor to save a pregnant woman's life. By the early 1970s several unsuccessful attempts had been made in the Texas legislature to liberalize the statute, but it remained firmly in place—until it became the bone of contention in *Roe v. Wade.*

7

A Memorable Garage Sale

Early one Friday morning in the autumn of 1967 two students from the University of Texas made a secret trip from Austin to Eagle Pass, Texas, on the Mexican border. One was Sarah Ragle, the other Ron Weddington, whom she planned to marry. After checking into a motel, they walked over the border into Piedras Negras where they had made arrangements for Sarah to have an abortion.

Sarah and Ron, both twenty-one years old, had met on a blind date not long before. Sarah was nearly finished with law school. Ron, whose education had been interrupted by the military draft, expected to receive his undergraduate degree the following summer, then enter law school. They had fallen in love and were talking of marriage when Sarah found to her distress that she was pregnant. Their finances and careers ruled out having a child at that time, so they decided Sarah should have an abortion, something she had never dreamed would happen to her. Above all she wanted it to remain secret, especially from her father, a Methodist minister, and her mother, a schoolteacher.

Abortion was illegal in Texas, so Ron quickly investigated

how they could arrange an abortion elsewhere. At the time, the Clergy Consultation Service, which might have helped, was not represented in Austin, but a local minister who approved of the service helped Ron find and telephone a reputable doctor performing abortions in Mexico, a doctor who had been educated in the United States and could provide a safe procedure in his well-equipped clinic. The couple drove to Eagle Pass that Friday for an appointment Sarah had with the doctor for an abortion later in the day.

Once across the border in Piedras Negras they kept a prearranged rendezvous with a man who led them through narrow, unpaved streets to a small, white building housing the clinic. The doctor and the cleanliness of his clinic put Sarah at ease, and while Ron waited outside, she was taken into a small operating room, given a general anaesthetic, and the surgery was performed. When she had regained consciousness, but still felt woozy, she and Ron walked back to the motel. As her head cleared, Sarah was glad to know the nightmare was over without complications, and it could remain a secret between her and Ron forever. The next day in Austin they returned to their studies as if nothing had happened.

But in fact something of great consequence had happened. The trip to Piedras Negras could not be forgotten, nor would it remain a secret forever. The experience would help motivate Sarah in an amazing role she would play that drastically changed the history of abortion in the United States. The beginning of that role occurred two years later in a most banal setting—a garage sale.

In the interim Sarah finished law school with the same rapidity characteristic of all her education. It took her only two years and three months to acquire a law degree that usually required three years. Furthermore, she earned her way through law school as a hospital records librarian, a freelance typist, and an assistant housemother in the dorm where she lived. That academic record was reminiscent of her earlier schooling. Allowed to skip two grades, she had covered the usual twelve years of public school in ten. She entered college at age sixteen and graduated at nineteen, taking three years compared to the usual four. Still, she completed law school in the top quarter of her class, which had over one hundred men and only five women.

Once she had her law degree, Sarah and Ron were married, and she looked for work to support them while he completed law school. But her remarkable academic record suddenly seemed meaningless when she became the first of the five women law school graduates to be invited for an interview at a large Dallas law firm. The invitation seemed a great honor, until the interviewer revealed the firm had no intentions of hiring her, or, for that matter, any woman. His flimsy reasons included, for example, that she probably couldn't stand the profanity of the firm's male attorneys, or that the partners' wives would object to their husbands' associating with a woman lawyer. It didn't take long for Sarah Weddington to realize the invitation had only been a token to the "libbers" (the nickname for women liberationists) who were beginning to complain that law firms were discriminating against women lawyers.

After other such rejections, Weddington decided her gender would, indeed, make a position in the all-male legal world more than she could stand. But she needed a job, and luckily one of her professors offered her a job assisting him on a project for a special committee of the American Bar Association. She accepted and went to work revising a document governing the ethical standards for lawyers. For Weddington the job provided badly needed income, but, equally important, it left her time to pursue interests and activities she had missed during her demanding college days.

In later years she wrote, "There are moments in your life—'aha' moments—when, for whatever reason, you suddenly see the facts in a different light." And that happened to Weddington once she was released from simultaneously getting and paying for an education. Her freedom to experience the kinds of things she'd missed provided new perspectives on her life. She later recalled them as having had "the most significant impact on my future as a lawyer." Chances are her career would have been entirely different had it started in a law firm like those that turned her down. In all likelihood her male colleagues would have stressed what a young woman should not do as an attorney, while relying on their experience to teach what she *should* do. For Sarah Weddington that experience might not have been the best teacher.

In her new freedom she was especially influenced by Judy Smith whom she met through one of Ron's classmates, Jim Wheelis. Smith had majored in chemistry at Brandeis University in Waltham, Massachusetts, and was now working on her doctorate in molecular biology at the University of Texas. An active participant in the developing feminist movement of the 1960s, she introduced Weddington to "consciousness-raising groups." There she met other new friends and found them concerned about the kinds of injustices she had encountered in the attitudes of all-male law firms. In the group meetings Weddington's "energy began to flow," as she described it, and she became incensed to think of the depth and pervasiveness of this injustice and how so many women accepted it, even in their most routine affairs.

She was struck by this phenomenon one day when she applied for a bank credit card. The banker told her he could not approve the card unless her husband signed the application. She objected, pointing out that she was a lawyer, a person in her own right even though married. No matter: the banker had to have the husband's signature, or no card. Sarah took the no-card alternative and left. It was another of many examples motivating her to help women overcome such discrimination.

Meanwhile several of her newfound friends were writing articles for "Austin's underground counterculture newspaper," namely *The Rag.* Such underground publications became a common journalistic phenomenon in the 1960s and early seventies, when young people, with their frank, outspoken questioning of America's widely accepted moral views, often raised the ire of those in power. *The Rag,* which devoted a lot of space to the rising tide of women's issues, incurred the wrath of the University of Texas's regents, and they forbade the sale of the paper on campus. A local attorney, along with Ron Weddington and Jim Wheelis, helped the students sue the university, claiming that the regents' ban of *The Rag* violated their rights to a free press under the First Amendment to the U.S. Constitution. The case went all the way up to the U.S. Supreme Court, which ruled for the students and forced the regents to lift their ban.

The newspaper then became even more forthright, giving

added attention to subjects that were taboo for the conventional media. These included open, frank information on birth-control methods and devices, still hard to come by in the Lone Star State. Boldest of all were articles on abortion, with practical advice for women, married or single, on how to obtain safe abortions, despite the Texas law making them illegal. Ron and Sarah Weddington, their secret still fresh in their minds, were especially appreciative of how important such help could be in the kind of predicament they had faced.

Then Judy Smith and Bea Durden, another of Sarah Weddington's new friends, helped organize a referral service advertised in *The Rag* as the Women's Liberation Birth Control Information Center. It had a telephone "hotline" which provided callers with home phone numbers of the center's counselors. The intent was to serve only women associated with the University of Texas, but as callers increased, many came from the Austin metropolitan area, as well as the university community.

The center's organizers agreed that their main goal was encouraging women to avoid unwanted pregnancies by birth-control methods for which the service could provide counseling. But as expected, many callers were seeking ways of terminating pregnancies. The center did not advertise abortion counseling, although the advertisements carried warnings about the hazards of unsafe abortions, self-performed or carried out by unqualified providers for exorbitant fees. Despite not advertising the service, the Women's Liberation Center did, in fact, help women find safe abortions performed by qualified doctors for reasonable prices. Such doctors were actively sought out and appraised by volunteers from the center. Approved physicians were mostly in Mexico, but a few were in Texas performing the surgery regardless of its illegality.

Around this time, the national Clergy Consultation Service formed an Austin chapter which cooperated with the Women's Liberation Center. The joint venture opened up many more possibilities for the Texas counselors to recommend abortion providers in and outside the United States. The expanding services and increasing numbers of women using them required more volunteer help and funds to pay the rising expenses. The money was raised, usually in small amounts, by various means. One productive method was the "garage sale": selling donated items.

One such sale was held on a fall Saturday in 1969 at a house in Austin where Ron and Sarah Weddington were renting one half the residence, including a garage in which the items to be sold had been stored. That morning Sarah Weddington, with Judy Smith and Bea Durden, took the sale's first two-hour shift, and they had plenty of time to talk between customers. What was said, not what was sold, made this event a turning point in Sarah Weddington's life, one that she would always remember.

Judy Smith, ordinarily a quiet, reserved person, talked at length about something troubling her very much. She pointed out that the Liberation Center's abortion counseling, despite its not being advertised, had become more visible to the public—and possibly to the police. Some of the volunteers were increasingly concerned that by helping women circumvent the Texas abortion law they might be in violation of it themselves and could be arrested. Smith didn't know if this was a serious threat or not, but she feared that one day the Austin police might suddenly appear and arrest everyone. Bea Durden confessed she'd had the same fear.

As the conversation continued, Smith and Durden obviously looked to Sarah Weddington, the only lawyer in their organization. Were they breaking the law simply by educating women about abortion? And what about their referring pregnant women to doctors for abortions? Was that illegal? Weddington—despite having made the secret trip to Mexico because of the Texas law—had to admit she knew little about it. Furthermore, she had encountered virtually nothing about abortion in law school. But, her friends asked, couldn't she do some research on how it might affect the counseling program they'd put so much into? She worked in the university law building with easy access to the law library. Moreover, they knew her ethical standards project was winding down, allowing her more time to work on her own.

Before their turn running the garage sale ended, Weddington agreed to look into what was worrying her friends. She went right to work in the law library, and what she found took her far beyond the question raised at the garage sale. In fact, she became so caught up in what she discovered about the legal status of abortion that she went deeper and deeper into the research, and it led her all the way to the Supreme Court of the United States. This is why, in an autobiography published thirty-three years later, Sarah Weddington wrote: "*Roe v. Wade* started at a garage sale, amid paltry castoffs."

8

A Meeting at Columbo's Pizza

Later that fall, Sarah Weddington spent as much time as possible in the university law library doing research on abortion law. One day she suddenly left the reading room and hurried around the building looking for her husband, Ron, who was still in law school. She couldn't wait to tell him what she had just found in *U.S. Reports,* the published decisions of the Supreme Court of the United States. Ron had become involved in Sarah's research, and she wanted to tell him immediately about a 1965 decision she had just read, *Griswold v. Connecticut.* The case's majority opinion, written by Justice William O. Douglas, had, in a flash, opened up a new perspective on what Weddington had been thinking of doing. She was particularly excited by the justice's statement, "We deal with a right of privacy older than the Bill of Rights—older than our political parties, older than our school system." The idea of a right to privacy, now granted constitutional protection by *Griswold,* made all the difference in the world to what Sarah Weddington had in mind. She had seriously started to think of suing the state of Texas in hopes of overturning its abortion law. When she found Ron, he, too, was excited, for he immediately caught on to the importance of her discovery.

The research that led Weddington to *Griswold v. Connecticut* began right after she had agreed to review the Texas abortion law for her worried friends. She soon concluded that little was to be learned about the law's possible use because it had been invoked in very few cases over its 115-year life. With this scarcity of "case law," it was difficult to say if her friends' abortion counseling might lead to arrests and prosecutions.

To consider the question from a broader point of view, Weddington looked at abortion decisions from other states and quickly found that antiabortion statutes were being challenged around the country. Indeed, one of the most important cases had just been decided in California, and more to the point of Weddington's interest, the case, *People v. Belous,* involved the referral of a woman for an illegal abortion.

In 1967 Dr. Leon P. Belous, a well-known Beverly Hills gynecologist, was convicted under California's antiabortion law for having referred a pregnant college student to a Mexican doctor who was doing abortions in California without an American license. The gynecologist's case was appealed to the California Supreme Court where, on September 5, 1969, seven judges voted, four to three, to overturn the conviction, declaring that the state law was "unconstitutionally vague." Lawyers all across the country felt that the precedent of *People v. Belous* left many state abortion laws vulnerable to attack.

In view of what she was learning, Weddington and her friends reversed their thinking about the Texas law, from what it might do to them to what they might do to it. The turnabout made her task far more formidable. It was even hard for her to imagine that she—a legal neophyte, and a woman at that—might bring down such a long-established state law. But those who knew Sarah Weddington realized she thrived on challenges. Her educational history testified to that, and here was a big challenge she was likely to meet—although at this point she hadn't the slightest idea of how immense it would become.

On November 10, 1969, along came another case that added to her developing interest in the fate of the nation's abortion laws. It was that of Dr. Milan Vuitch, a Serbian-born doctor who had been performing hundreds of illegal abortions in Washington, D.C. He had finally been arrested for violating the District of Columbia's antiabortion law, adopted around the turn of the century, and was awaiting trial, not in a state court but in a federal court because the District of Columbia was federal territory. But with Vuitch's prosecution still pending, a well-known federal district court judge, Gerhard A. Gesell, dismissed the case. He supported his action with the same reasoning used by the California Supreme Court in *Belous*: Judge Gesell held that the District of Columbia statute was "unconstitutionally vague." Dr. Vuitch returned to his abortion business, and the Gesell decision was hailed around the country as another sign that the days of state abortion laws were numbered.

At this time Sarah Weddington was also influenced by what her husband and his classmate Jim Wheelis were learning about the federal court system, and they began to see the possibilities it held for a case against the Texas abortion law. Judy Smith, who was party to their discussions, decided the federal courts were the way to go, not only to overturn the Texas law, but possibly with one stroke to overturn many such laws across the country. She urged Weddington to consider taking their case into the federal courts, assuring her she was capable of doing it.

The thought of tackling such an ambitious case was awesome, and Weddington brought up all the reasons she could think of to convince her husband and friends it was far beyond her. She later confessed to having had an unspoken reason to avoid such a case, simply the fear that she might fail. She had never experienced failure, and the possibility frightened her. However, this was offset by a belief inherited from her parents, that it was important to contribute to the common good—of women, in this case. Personal finances were also a consideration because her legal work had to be *pro bono publico.* She and Ron decided they could get along with what savings they had until the following summer (of 1971). Finally, at a dinner in their apartment with Judy Smith and Jim Wheelis, Sarah agreed she would give a try at challenging the Texas antiabortion law in federal court.

She already had an idea of how best to proceed. She was fairly certain the initial complaint should be filed with a "three-judge court" (a court formed specifically to deal with a single case challenging the constitutionality of a state law). The three judges would be drawn from two divisions of the federal judicial system. One would come from the Fifth Circuit Court of Appeals headquartered in New Orleans and covering Texas (it being at that time one of the eleven circuits, or judicial areas, in the United States). This "circuit judge" would then appoint two other judges from the lower federal district courts located within his circuit. Finally the threesome would meet to hear the case. This special, temporarily formed kind of court had been established early in the century but seldom used until revived by civil rights lawyers in the 1960s. They recognized that by lumping together two main divisions of the federal system the three-judge court often offered the most direct route for bringing a case up to the U.S. Supreme Court located directly above. Subsequently the number of these special courts increased dramatically.

Of course a lawyer had to know a great deal about the procedures required to bring together the three judges to hear a case. This was where Sarah Weddington needed help, and she had an idea that a law school classmate, Linda Coffee, could provide it.

Coffee had also been a star performer throughout her school years, including law school from which she graduated with honors. When she took the Texas bar examination (required to become a practicing attorney) she tied for the second highest score in the state. Two months later, in June 1968, Coffee became a law clerk for a well-known federal judge, Sarah Hughes. (Judge Hughes had been seen on television by millions of people administering the oath of office to Lyndon B. Johnson on *Air Force One* after the assassination of President Kennedy.) Coffee's one-year clerking for Sarah Hughes provided valuable experience with the federal court system—including special three-judge courts. After the clerkship she went to work at a small Dallas law firm. She had been there about eight months when, on December 3, 1969, she received a telephone call from Sarah Weddington.

Weddington said she needed help with a case aimed at overturning the Texas abortion law. Would Coffee help? Coffee liked the idea but needed to think it over and see how her law firm would react. She soon called back to say the firm had no objections and she was ready to help. Weddington and Coffee met briefly in Dallas, then conversed a lot by telephone between Austin and Dallas, mostly about finding a plaintiff for the lawsuit. Initially they thought of using the women's abortion counseling service, but it would be hard to prove that the organization had legal "standing" (meaning legalistically that a party is sufficiently affected by a controversy to expect a court to resolve it). The two young lawyers decided the strongest case could be made with a pregnant woman prevented by the Texas law from having an abortion that she needed and wanted. Such a plaintiff would undoubtedly have legal standing, but locating the right person seemed like finding a needle in a haystack.

Right after New Year's, 1970, Coffee called from Dallas; she had found a prospective plaintiff, a young, pregnant woman. Unable to obtain an abortion, she had gone to a lawyer to prearrange an adoption for the baby. The lawyer, having learned of Coffee's possible challenge to the law, suggested the woman call her. She did, thinking it might lead to an abortion. Coffee met her briefly, then called Weddington to come from Austin and meet the woman.

The meeting, one of the more fateful in the annals of American law, took place in Dallas on Mockingbird Lane at Columbo's Pizza—which had been recommended by the prospective plaintiff and was fine with the lawyers, both of whom were working for free and so didn't have much money to spare.

"Columbo's is gone now, which is a shame," the woman, Norma McCorvey, wrote twenty-four years later. "The tables had red-and-white-checked tablecloths—just like the one I'd bought for Woody [her former husband back in California]. Columbo's wasn't very big. When I walked into the place that evening, I didn't have any trouble figuring out who was waiting for me.

"Linda Coffee and Sarah Weddington, sitting together, stood out in Columbo's. Both were older than me, and both were wearing two-piece business suits. Nice clothing, expensive-looking. . . . I was wearing jeans, a button-down shirt tied at the waist, and sandals. I wore my bandanna tied around my left leg, above my knee. That meant I didn't have a girlfriend."

McCorvey came there, nervous and unsure of what the meeting was about, but still hoping the two lawyers might have some way of helping her out of the problems her pregnancy was certain to cause. Coffee and Weddington saw her as a thin waif worn with troubles. And, indeed, McCorvey had many tales of woe. She told about some, left out others, and stressed an important one that, years later, she would confess was a lie.

Norma Leah Nelson (her family name) was born on September 22, 1947, to troubled parents who were divorced when she was thirteen. She dropped out of high school and, at age sixteen, while working as a carhop in a drive-in, she met and soon married twenty-four-year-old Woody McCorvey, a twice-divorced, unemployed sheet-metal worker. Looking for a job, Woody took his bride to his parents' home in Pasadena, California, then moved to Los Angeles. Norma liked to sing along with songs she heard on the radio, and Woody, praising the quality of her voice, claimed he could get her a recording contract in Hollywood that would lead to stardom. But this great hope ended one day when Norma revealed she was pregnant. The enraged husband, claiming the pregnancy could not have been by him, beat her up, and the terrorized Norma fled back to Dallas. The baby, a girl, was born and named

Melissa, but the mother was unable to care for the tiny daughter, so her mother, living in Louisiana with a new husband, adopted Melissa. Then came a second pregnancy, this one out of wedlock. A prearranged adoption resulted in the baby's being taken from the mother at birth.

Now, as McCorvey ate her pizza at Columbo's, she didn't reveal this past life but talked only of the current pregnancy. It was some two months in progress, and she hoped the two lawyers could arrange an abortion. A friend had told her it might help to claim she had been raped. Well, had she been raped? Yes, she said. But she really hadn't. It was a lie to which years later she would confess. She told the lawyers she had been working with a traveling carnival in Louisiana (true), and one night she had been attacked and raped (untrue). But true or false it made no difference to the lawyers, and they told her so, because the Texas abortion law made no exception for rape.

Then, to her disappointment, McCorvey learned that Coffee and Weddington could not help her get an abortion. Surprising as it seemed to her, they were planning something that might help all Texas women in her situation to be free to have abortions. Still hoping that what they were up to might somehow help her, she expressed interest in why the lawyers wanted to see her. They explained that possibly she might become a plaintiff—a word McCorvey didn't know—in a court case to overturn the law that now kept her from having a safe, affordable abortion. Could this, she asked innocently, allow her to have an abortion before it would be too late? No. The case couldn't possibly be won in that short a time.

But as the three women ate their pizzas, McCorvey's troubled life and lack of sophistication became increasingly evident, raising doubts with Coffee and Weddington about the sad young woman's dependability as a plaintiff. However, she began to warm up to the idea of playing a role in such an important lawsuit, and she asked more questions. How much would the lawyers charge her? Nothing! They were working for free for the public interest. Would Norma's name be involved? Not necessarily. In fact it might be best if she went by an anonymous name.

When they had finished dinner and were getting ready to pay the bill, McCorvey agreed to become a plaintiff. The lawyers expressed their appreciation but remained nervous about the woman. They left Columbo's saying they had to make more arrangements and would telephone her soon. Later they agreed that allowing a week or two before calling might test the seriousness of McCorvey's off-the-cuff decision to play the key part in the case.

Meanwhile, Coffee and Weddington found another possible plaintiff, Marsha King, who had heard Coffee speak about their case. King had suggested she might be a plaintiff and explained why. When she was married in 1968, she used the relatively new birth-control pill that had proven effective for millions of women, only to find it had very serious side effects for her. On a doctor's recommendation she changed to a diaphragm, but that failed and the resulting pregnancy caused her such serious physical and mental problems that her husband, John, rushed her to a Mexico City clinic for an abortion. Marsha King was then diagnosed as suffering from a neurochemical disorder and warned not to use the birth-control pill and not to get pregnant. Unless she and her husband abstained from sex, which they didn't want to do, they were left at the mercy of a diaphragm which had already proven ineffective. They wanted no more Mexican abortions, and the Texas law forbade Marsha from having a safe, dependable abortion near home. She felt she had reason to challenge the law.

While the Kings' dilemma could be blamed on the state law, Coffee and Weddington were not sure it would provide them with legal standing as the plaintiffs the lawyers needed. They feared the question of standing would undoubtedly arise, given that King was not currently pregnant and confronted with its serious consequences. However, thinking it over, they decided a case with both John and Marsha King as plaintiffs might work—if the legal-standing question could be resolved. The Kings agreed to serve anonymously, and their case, when filed, was titled *John and Mary Doe v. Henry Wade.*

A couple of weeks after meeting Norma McCorvey at Columbo's Pizza, Coffee telephoned her, prepared to find she had disappeared. But McCorvey answered the telephone, saying she'd had no success arranging an abortion, and she definitely wanted to become a plaintiff. When she came to Coffee's office to sign the necessary papers, McCorvey liked the first anonymous name they had given her, "Jane," but not the last, "Doe." Coffee solved that by simply changing the *D* to an *R*, and the new plaintiff became Jane Roe. The defendant was someone McCorvey had never heard of, Henry Wade, despite his being well known in Dallas. The actual title of McCorvey's case became *Jane Roe, Plaintiff, v. Henry Wade, District Attorney of Dallas County, Defendant.* Or, for short, *Roe v. Wade.*

9

Two "Genteel Southern Ladies" Are Good Lawyers

On March 3, 1970, Linda Coffee walked to the Dallas Federal Courthouse, went to the clerk's office, filed the cases of Jane Roe and John and Mary Doe, and paid the $30 fee, in cash from her own pocket. Except for the facts describing the plaintiffs, the two cases were identical. They asked for the appointment of a three-judge court to hear their complaints claiming the Texas abortion statute violated the plaintiffs' personal right to privacy secured by the First, Fourth, Fifth, Eighth, Ninth, and Fourteenth Amendments of the U.S. Constitution.

The heart of their argument rested on the right of privacy established by *Griswold v. Connecticut.* While *Griswold* had not been about abortion, the new *Roe* and *Doe* complaints quoted from a recent *Loyola University Law Review* article that drew the connection. The author, retired Supreme Court justice Tom C. Clark, had voted for *Griswold.* Clark claimed that "abortion falls within that sensitive area of privacy—the marital relation [as established by the Connecticut case]." In addition to the privacy issue, Coffee and Weddington charged that the Texas law was so vague a doctor could not tell, with respect to abortion, what was actually against the law. Finally the lawyers asked that Henry Wade be ordered to stop enforcing the law (if the judges declared it unconstitutional).

The filing of the abortion cases immediately came to the attention of a young Dallas lawyer, Roy Merrill, who represented a physician, James H. Hallford of Carrollton, recently indicted under the Texas law for performing abortions. Merrill, who had intended to challenge the law's constitutionality, contacted Coffee and suggested the doctor become another plaintiff with the *Roe-Doe* plaintiffs. She was delighted to add a medical plaintiff, which the court allowed, and on March 23 Merrill filed the doctor's complaint.

Shortly thereafter, Coffee and Weddington became aware of a deficiency in their complaints already filed with the court. They had assumed winning their cases would benefit women in comparable circumstances everywhere but belatedly found that wouldn't necessarily be true, unless the complaints had been filed as "class actions" specifying they were, in fact, acting for all women. But in their rush the two lawyers had overlooked this possibility. Hoping to remedy the oversight, Weddington called on her former constitutional law professor, who explained how it could be corrected by amending the complaints. Moreover, she learned this change would take care of a worry over what would happen when Jane Roe's pregnancy ended with the birth of a child and Henry Wade argued she no longer had legal standing. A class action would undercut Wade's argument because somewhere at any given time there would be one or more pregnant women faced with Jane Roe's problem. The appropriate amendment was submitted to the court, which agreed to *Roe v. Wade*'s becoming a class action.

Meanwhile the three judges for the special court had been chosen. They included District Judge Sarah Hughes, for whom Linda Coffee had clerked, District Judge William Taylor, and Dallas resident circuit judge, Irving Goldberg.

When the defendant, Henry Wade, received the complaints, he paid no special attention—abortion cases had never interested him anyway. Wade was an extremely busy public official with over a hundred attorneys to supervise. The attorney who did have to pay attention was thirty-six-year-old John B. Tolle, the head of Wade's division responsible for federal cases. When Tolle saw that the cases came from Linda Coffee, he was surprised. He had gained respect for Coffee when she clerked for Sarah Hughes, and now he wondered how she'd become mixed up with such an "oddball thing." However, her name made him realize that the cases were not frivolous.

Tolle's first formal response to the complaints was brief and technical. He claimed Jane Roe lacked legal standing because the Texas abortion statute concerned only persons who performed abortions, not pregnant women. Another of Wade's attorneys, Wilson Johnston, responded to John and Mary Doe's complaint. He proposed that since Mary Doe was not pregnant and might never be, she and her husband were not in conflict with the abortion law. Their case, he suggested, was only an effort to obtain advice from the court on how the law might or might not be enforced.

More than two and a half months after the initial papers had been filed, the three cases were finally heard by the three-judge court. The hearing, held in Sarah Hughes's courtroom, was called to order by Circuit Judge Irving Goldberg at two P.M., on May 22, 1970. The room was crowded with women supporting the plaintiffs. Jane Roe, whose pregnancy was now very evident, did not attend, but John and Mary Doe were present. Six attorneys were there, four for the plaintiffs, including Dr. Hallford's, and two from Wade's office sent to defend the law. The total time allotted for the attorneys had been divided equally among the six who would address the court—thirteen minutes each.

Linda Coffee spoke first and began by contesting the state's argument that the *Roe* and *Doe* plaintiffs did not have standing. She then contended that the Texas abortion law violated the Constitution of the United States by denying her plaintiffs' rights to personal privacy protected by the six constitutional amendments cited in the complaints. But she had barely mentioned the First Amendment when both Sarah Hughes and Irving Goldberg interrupted and pressed her to talk about the Ninth Amendment. However, her effort to comply was frequently interrupted by the two judges asking questions and commenting on the answers. To Coffee's distress her planned presentation became disjointed, and the first thing she knew her allotted thirteen minutes were up.

Sarah Weddington's turn came next, and she never forgot that moment—as she recalled a quarter century later: "I was twenty-five years old; I had never argued in a contested case, and it was my first appearance before federal judges. My voice quivered. Sarah Hughes looked down at me from the bench; she could see how nervous I was. She gave me a reassuring smile and a slight wink, as if to say, 'Don't be nervous. Everything will be fine.' . . . I took it as an older woman lawyer's remembering what it was like when she was starting out."

Weddington recovered from her initial stage fright and did

remarkably well, despite Judge Goldberg's testy interruptions. She pressed the issue of women's right to privacy, only to have the circuit judge ask if the state had any right to regulate abortion. She answered yes, but only after the point in a pregnancy when the fetus can survive outside of the mother's body. Prior to that time, Weddington maintained, a woman has the right to an abortion as a matter of personal privacy, a right protected by the Ninth Amendment to the Constitution. Judge Goldberg asked if the Texas law's vulnerability was greater because it violated the Ninth Amendment right or because of its vagueness. Weddington firmly chose the Ninth Amendment. Her thirteen minutes were soon up, and it was clear that the neophyte had done exceedingly well.

Dr. Hallford's two attorneys came next, and, as agreed to with Coffee and Weddington, they concentrated on the vagueness issue, as cited in the recent California and District of Columbia decisions, *Belous* and *Vuitch.* The Texas law was so vague, they claimed, that a doctor couldn't possibly know what legally he could or could not do in regard to abortion. Leaning on the *Belous* and *Vuitch* decisions, the Hallford attorneys argued that the Texas law their plaintiff was up against should be declared "unconstitutionally vague."

Henry Wade's side of the case supporting the abortion law was argued by John Tolle and Jay Floyd, another of Wade's attorneys. As they proceeded, making their case largely on technical grounds, it became clear from the three judges' reactions that the state's case was not doing well.

Floyd argued that Jane Roe didn't have legal standing because her pregnancy had [by that date] progressed beyond the time when she could safely have an abortion. Judge Hughes pointed out that *Roe* was a class action certain to involve many women in early pregnancies who would have standing. So Floyd's argument didn't hold water. He then tried to demolish Jane Roe's case, saying the right to abortion was not found anywhere in the Constitution, leading Judge Goldberg to ask Floyd to talk about the Ninth Amendment and the right to privacy. Clearly unable to do so, the lawyer responded by attempting to change the subject. All told, he hadn't done very well before his time expired.

During much of John Tolle's time, he argued that the right of an unborn child to life was more important than a woman's right to privacy. It was a hard case to make, and the judges were not impressed. At the close of his presentation, the hearing ended.

The judges retired to a small library off the courtroom and met for only a few minutes—but a fateful few. They agreed with the *Roe v. Wade* plaintiffs that the Texas abortion law was unconstitutional. Judge Hughes was chosen to write the decision for all three judges. But then a most important point had to be resolved when Sarah Hughes asked her colleagues if the decision should grant the request Coffee and Weddington had included in the *Roe* complaint—that the court order Henry Wade to cease enforcing the abortion law now that they were declaring it unconstitutional. Hughes was for it, but Judge Goldberg objected. He could see how the order might lead the state to appeal their decision to the U.S. Supreme Court. That, he feared, could very well result in the Court's reversal of the decision they had just agreed on. He based his assumption on the fact that the High Court had recently reversed lower-court decisions ordering states to take such actions. The circuit judge's advice was accepted, and the *Roe v. Wade* decision said nothing as to what Wade should do. As it turned out, if Coffee and Weddington's request had been granted, *Roe v. Wade* might have been rejected by the Supreme Court for a reason unrelated to abortion and become a minor footnote in history.

The decision written by Sarah Hughes for the court and handed down on June 17, 1970, was unusually brief, less than nine printed pages. It agreed that while Jane Roe and Dr. Hallford had the legal standing to challenge the Texas abortion law, John and Mary Doe did not. To the main point made in the *Roe v. Wade* complaint—that the Texas law denied women their right under the Ninth Amendment to choose whether or not to have children—the decision simply said, "We agree." They also agreed to overrule Dr. Hallford's indictment.

The loser, Henry Wade, was evidently unswayed by the decision. "Apparently we're free to try them [violators of the abortion law], so we'll still do so," he said when he learned that the court had given him no orders. That announcement turned out to be a great favor to Linda Coffee and Sarah Weddington. It was open sesame for *Roe v. Wade* to go directly and immediately to the Supreme Court of the United States. The justices have to pay attention when a state official intends to continue using a law declared unconstitutional by a lower federal court.

The initial victory of *Roe v. Wade* caught the media's attention all over Texas and made headlines in leading newspapers across the country. The story was all the more newsworthy because two young female attorneys had won the case. "If their day in court proves anything," the *Houston Post* said, "it certainly proves that genteel Southern ladies can indeed be very good lawyers."

The Texas case immediately assumed an important role among several abortion cases with the potential for going up to the nation's highest court. One of these cases was remarkably similar to *Roe v. Wade.* It was already under way in Georgia where another "southern lady" attorney, Margie Pitts Hames, was representing the pregnant, twenty-two-year-old Sandra Bensing, already the mother of three children who were not in her custody. Bensing's marriage was as troubled as could be, her husband having left her broke and pregnant. When Margie Hames took over, the deeply distressed woman had tried but failed to obtain a "therapeutic" abortion to prevent bringing a fourth child into her terrible family situation. Georgia's new, liberalized abortion law was a product of the nation's reform effort, but it still rejected cases like Sandra Bensing's. In her behalf Margie Hames brought a case challenging the new law. Sandra Bensing became Mary Doe, the plaintiff, and Georgia's attorney general, Arthur K. Bolton, became the defendant. Only three weeks after *Roe v. Wade* had been heard by the three-judge federal court in Texas, *Doe v. Bolton* was heard by a three-judge federal court in Georgia. And some six weeks after Coffee and Weddington's *Roe* victory, their Atlanta counterpart won her *Doe* case, and the new Georgia abortion law was declared unconstitutional. As was true with *Roe,* the *Doe* decision avoided including an order for Arthur Bolton to cease enforcing the law, thus providing another direct move to the U.S. Supreme Court.

Informed observers felt the Supreme Court might find it attractive to take the Texas and Georgia cases as a pair. It would allow the justices to consider (1) an old state abortion law typical of many still outlawing abortion in the United

States, with (2) a newly reformed statute liberalizing but not completely repealing antiabortion laws.

Coffee and Weddington heard not only from compatriots like Margie Hames but also from possible assistants among the growing number of persons and organizations advocating repeal of state abortion laws. One of the most attractive offers came from a young New York attorney, Roy Lucas, who had formed the James Madison Constitutional Law Institute, devoted to repeal of abortion laws. In early 1970 Lucas was responsible for an important case, *Hall v. Lefkowitz,* which challenged the constitutionality of New York State's abortion law. It had the potential for going on appeal to the U.S. Supreme Court and possibly leading to a landmark decision overturning all state abortion laws. But on April 11, 1970, Lucas's case abruptly became moot (no longer of legal significance) when the statute he challenged was repealed by the state legislature, and abortion became legal in New York. The energetic Lucas, with his Madison Institute, looked around the nation for abortion cases where he could help. He contacted both Coffee and Weddington in Texas and Hames in Georgia, virtually offering to take over and bring their cases up to the Supreme Court. Hames found him too pushy and declined his help in favor of doing the job herself. However, in Texas his assistance was accepted by Coffee and Weddington, whose financial situations made the help from New York welcome. Lucas then took the lead in preparing and filing the early submissions required to take *Roe v. Wade* on appeal to the High Court.

That summer and fall of 1970, Coffee and Weddington dealt with financial problems that had accumulated because of the free time they'd devoted to *Roe v. Wade.* Coffee faced a large backlog of work that had piled up at her law firm, and it fully occupied her for a long time. Ron Weddington, who had graduated from law school, found a position with a Fort Worth law firm, and he and Sarah moved there from Austin. She landed a job as an assistant city attorney, becoming the first female ever to hold the position. Meanwhile she used her time off to contribute to the continuing effort of Texas women lobbying the state legislature to repeal the abortion law—in case the *Roe v. Wade* appeal should fail to do so.

10

From the Warren Court to the Burger Court

From the inception of *Roe v. Wade,* Linda Coffee and Sarah Weddington had concentrated on winning a decision in the federal three-judge court against the nineteenth-century Texas statute. When they won, and it seemed *Roe* might be going to the U.S. Supreme Court, they began to worry about the Court's recent changes in membership and philosophy that could affect the outcome of their appeal. What little Coffee and Weddington had learned from news reports in recent months gave them reason to fear the Court would favor Henry Wade.

In 1969 and 1970 the High Court went through a historic upheaval starting shortly before Weddington began the library research that eventually led her and Coffee to *Roe v. Wade.* The disturbance in Washington occurred as the "Warren Court" became the "Burger Court."

Chief Justice Earl Warren led the Court from 1953 to June 23, 1969. In discussing Warren's background, Bernard Schwartz, the historian of the Supreme Court, observed, "There have been scholars and there have been justices on the Supreme Court. But scholars have not always been great justices, and the great justices have not always been scholars."

Earl Warren did not pretend to be a scholar, but undeniably he became one of the Court's greatest justices. He was mainly a politician, having become the only California governor elected to three terms. In 1953 President Dwight D. Eisenhower appointed Warren to replace Chief Justice Fred M. Vinson, who had died in office.

The new chief quickly applied the leadership qualities he had demonstrated in politics. He turned to two of the Court's activists, Justices Black and Douglas—both Roosevelt appointees from the 1930s—and in the next fifteen years they helped Warren lead the Court through a historic era marked by its unusual activism that forced states to make numerous changes in their laws. Its decisions became extremely controversial and, in the eyes of the Court's many critics, turned the justices into legislators when they should have confined themselves to being judges.

The Warren Court's great centerpiece decision came down in 1954, only a year after the new chief's arrival: *Brown v. Board of Education,* the school desegregation case that forced the end of separate schools for white and black students. *Brown* became one of the most controversial decisions in the Court's entire history given the tremendous impact it had, especially across the South. The decision kindled the powerful civil rights movement challenging deeply ingrained laws and social customs, and it opened the way for civil rights lawyers to bring case after case before the Supreme Court to overrule state laws still supporting segregation.

As this turmoil continued, the Warren Court struck at another sensitive area of state laws, that of dealing with criminal justice. Becoming more and more controversial, Chief Justice

Warren led his Court to consider and rule on what he felt was a badly needed degree of fairness in such matters as police conduct, arrest procedures, search and seizure of evidence, and the treatment of suspects. From these concerns came several landmark decisions. Their unpopularity with many of the nation's police helped make Earl Warren one of the most controversial chief justices in the Court's history. Two public appraisals of the man revealed how sharply divided were feelings for and against him. In 1966 Vice President Hubert Humphrey said if President Eisenhower had done nothing else in his career, his appointment of Warren as chief justice "would have earned [the president] a very important place in the history of the United States." However, Eisenhower himself declared that the appointment was "the biggest damn-fool mistake I ever made."

In 1968 Warren told President Johnson he wanted to retire, but would wait until his replacement had been found and confirmed. The president nominated Justice Abe Fortas to take Warren's seat; however, the nominee, who had been an old friend of Johnson's, encountered serious problems in the Senate. His confirmation was delayed and delayed until finally the president withdrew the nomination, leaving Fortas a justice instead of the chief.

Meanwhile, Richard M. Nixon won the 1968 election and became president in January 1969. The chief justice's wish to resign was then passed along to President Nixon, who had been one of Warren's harshest critics. He now had an opportunity to keep a campaign promise and start reversing Warren's liberal record by appointing conservatives to the Court as the occasion arose. However, Nixon didn't hurry, and four months later Chief Justice Warren still headed the Court.

Then, in the first days of May 1969, the High Court was badly shaken when a *Life* magazine article exposed the problem that may have kept the Senate from confirming Abe Fortas as chief justice. *Life* claimed that Justice Fortas had unwisely accepted $20,000 from the family foundation of a man then in prison for stock manipulation. Justice Fortas claimed he had returned the money, but still the controversy led the man who might have become chief to resign from the Court.

Now the new president had a chance to replace two Supreme Court liberals, Earl Warren and Abe Fortas, with conservatives of his choice, and in less than a week he nominated a new chief justice, Warren E. Burger.

The nominee, a Minnesotan, had been serving in the District of Columbia on the federal Court of Appeals where his voting record indicated he was the kind of jurist Richard Nixon had promised in his campaign. Judge Burger was, in the president's opinion, the kind of conservative needed to replace one of the most liberal chiefs in history. What's more, Warren Burger looked like a Hollywood casting director's choice for the country's top judge: a kindly, imposing figure with broad shoulders and a shock of white, wavy hair. By the end of June 1969, the Senate had confirmed his nomination, the president had accepted Earl Warren's resignation, and Warren Burger had been sworn in as the new chief justice.

With that done smoothly and quickly, the president took his time finding Justice Fortas's replacement. Finally, in the middle of August, he nominated Judge Clement F. Haynsworth, Jr., from South Carolina, a member of the U.S. Circuit Court of Appeals. With this choice Richard Nixon stumbled badly. Judge Haynsworth was not only a conservative but also an extreme one, and a rising tide of opposition to him flooded the Senate for three months while the president tried but failed to save the nomination. Finally the Senate voted a record-making rejection of a Supreme Court nominee, the first since 1930, and with the largest vote margin in history: fifty-five to forty-five.

Two months later a bitter President Nixon sent the senators another nomination for the Fortas seat, this time federal judge G. Harrold Carswell of Tallahassee, Florida. Not only was he a conservative, he also had a reputation for mediocrity. The nomination opened the president to the charge that he was acting only for the political purpose of strengthening what had become known as his "southern strategy," and again the Senate, beset by three more months of opposition, rejected Carswell by a vote of fifty-one to forty-five.

His two failures left the widespread impression that the new president's contempt for the Warren Court's liberals had gotten out of hand. In almost one year in office, Nixon had succeeded with only one Supreme Court appointment, that of Chief Justice Warren Burger. But if Burger had been chosen as a conservative firebrand to undo the liberal activism of his predecessor, the flame had yet to be kindled. The new chief seemed mostly concerned with renovations and housekeeping in the Marble Palace (the nickname given the Court's new home opened in 1935). For example, under his direction the building's cafeteria was redecorated and supplied with new china and glassware of his choice. As if to stress his new exalted position, the chief had a carpet installed leading from his chambers to the justices' "robing room," hidden by red velvet drapes to the rear of the bench where the nine justices held court. One major change disturbed ardent devotees of the Court with memories going back to the 1930s, when the whiskered Chief Justice Charles Evans Hughes, Jr., sat at the center of the Court's long, straight bench. Warren Burger had it replaced with a winged bench, shaped like one side of a hexagon. Meanwhile, the president's hopes that the new chief would undo the work of the Warren Court were not to be quickly fulfilled—in fact, they didn't materialize in all of Warren Burger's seventeen years as chief.

However, his physical changes of the building signaled something of importance about the way Burger regarded his office. He had a deep respect for the Supreme Court as an institution, which would influence what he did there. He became very disturbed by the damaging ruckus caused by the president's flawed efforts to fill the Fortas seat, and he soon got word to the White House that it was time to stop flailing the Court. To help in that respect the chief justice recommended for nomination a conservative judge in Minnesota who, he predicted, would easily win Senate confirmation. The president took the advice, and promptly sent the recommended nomination to the Senate.

The Minnesotan was Harry A. Blackmun, a judge of the Eighth Circuit Court of Appeals. He was a longtime friend of Warren Burger's—indeed they had been classmates in grade school. As an undergraduate at Harvard University, he majored in mathematics and then went on to graduate from Harvard Law School in 1932. For a while he taught at Mitchell College of Law, Burger's alma mater, in St. Paul. He then became the "house lawyer" for the famous Mayo Clinic, and nine years later President Eisenhower appointed him to the federal Court of Appeals. The Senate took less than thirty days to confirm President Nixon's nomination, and on June 10, 1970, Harry Blackmun was sworn in as an associate justice of the Supreme Court. The president could finally say he had reduced the Warren Court liberals by two—but saying so didn't make it so, as history would prove.

One week to the day of Blackmun's swearing in, the case that would forever be tied to his name, *Roe v. Wade,* was decided by the three-judge court in Dallas. However, it took one year minus twenty-seven days before Linda Coffee and Sarah Weddington learned that the Supreme Court would hear their *Roe* appeal. During that time Roy Lucas met the October deadline for filing a jurisdictional statement, the document asking the High Court to consider the case, and everyone waited nervously for a reply. The wait, from fall to winter to spring, took some seven months.

Meanwhile, Coffee, Weddington, and everyone involved spent a lot of time wondering and worrying about the recent changes in the Supreme Court's membership. Most worrisome was the Court's apparent swing toward conservatism and "judicial restraint," which would avoid decisions forcing changes in state laws. If that were true, *Roe v. Wade* seemed certain to lose. The justices might well refuse to hear the appeal, leaving the three-judge court's decision unenforced and Henry Wade free to apply the Texas law as in the past. Or if the appeal were taken, the emerging, leave-the-states-alone conservatism could very well lead to a reversal of the *Roe* decision in Dallas, and that would be the end of *Roe v. Wade.*

Linda Coffee, Sarah Weddington, Roy Lucas, and everyone hoping for a *Roe* victory spent a lot of time trying to make objective, educated guesses as to how the nine sitting justices would vote on an abortion case. The best guide remained how six of those justices had voted on *Griswold v. Connecticut.* While *Griswold* was not about abortion, the decision established the constitutionally protected right to personal privacy, which was at the heart of the three-judge *Roe* decision in Texas. Four of the six had voted for *Griswold,* Justices Harlan, Brennan, White, and Douglas, who had written the *Griswold* majority opinion. Two of the six, Justices Black and Stewart, had voted against *Griswold,* leaving three members of the Burger Court with question marks: Burger, Blackmun, and Marshall. The educated guesses said that Justice Marshall would vote in favor of *Roe.* Thurgood Marshall, the first black ever appointed to the Court, had replaced Justice Tom Clark in 1967. For the two Nixon appointees, Burger and Blackmun, the guesses had them voting against *Roe.* If those who had favored *Griswold* held together to favor *Roe* and were joined by Justice Marshall, the Supreme Court's decision would come down against Henry Wade and the law he enforced.

But this conjecture depended on many "ifs" and became more puzzling in April 1971, when the Court announced its decision in *United States v. Vuitch,* by which the District of Columbia doctor was denied the right to continue his extensive abortion practice. The Court's majority opinion, written by Justice Black, was extremely complicated and confusing. At first the supporters of abortion felt it indicated a defeat for *Roe v. Wade,* and Linda Coffee and Sarah Weddington learned of the decision with dismay. However, other informed readers of the ten-page opinion reached a different conclusion, indicating a victory for *Roe.*

None of those concerned knew about something that happened the day following the announcement of the *Vuitch* decision. The justices—who had previously agreed among themselves to wait for the *Vuitch* decision before deciding whether or not to take two abortion cases waiting on appeal—*Roe v. Wade* from Texas and *Doe v. Bolton* from Georgia—voted, five to four, to hear both cases. However, this decision, reached in private, was not revealed for one month, not until May 21, 1971, when the Orders of the United States Supreme Court announced that *Roe v. Wade* from Texas and *Doe v. Bolton* from Georgia would be heard that fall on a date to be announced.

11

Nine Justices Become Seven

Everyone involved in *Roe v. Wade*—except Jane Roe, who couldn't be found—became ecstatic over the news from the Supreme Court. The long wait had caused Coffee and Weddington to fear their appeal would be rejected. So when *Roe* was accepted, they were stunned to think the Supreme Court of the United States was paying attention to them. Weddington's excitement was evident to everyone around her, including those in the office where she worked. But her joy was not shared by her boss who had taken pride in hiring her, the first female city attorney. Summoning her to his office, he handed her a sheet of paper on which he had inscribed seven words: "No more women's lib! No more abortion!" It was an ultimatum to comply or leave—possibly initiated by the city council. He said she could think it over. But after Sarah discussed the edict with Ron, her reply to the boss was to resign. Despite the financial strains it might cause them, the alternative, not working on the Supreme Court appeal, would have been insane.

Weddington called Roy Lucas in New York, who realized she would be extremely important in terms of preparing *Roe v. Wade* for the High Court. He offered her a part-time job to help make up her loss of income. His James Madison Constitutional Law Institute needed an office in the Southwest, and Weddington could run it while helping on the *Roe* case. Lucas said he was already drafting the petitioner's brief for delivery to the Supreme Court by the June 17 deadline. Weddington accepted the job, then waited for a copy of the brief which Lucas had promised to send. But it didn't show up and didn't show up, although Lucas repeated his promise to write it. She became anxious about missing the deadline for the delivery of the key document required by the Court. She expressed her concern to Coffee, who recalled having been warned about Lucas's inclination to take on more than he could handle, and they decided Weddington should fly to New York to find out what was going on.

When she arrived in the big city, for the first time in her life, she found the Madison Institute's all-male staff frantically following up on commitments Lucas had made with people and organizations around the country. When she asked to see the *Roe* brief, she was appalled to find it hadn't even been started. She was furious and decided, no question about it, to take over and go to work concentrating on *Roe*—which she did, despite Lucas's expecting her to help with his other projects.

First she prevailed on Lucas to request an extension of the Court's deadline. He did, and it was extended to August 17—two extra months, still not too much time. Weddington then found that before the petitioner's brief another submission was due at the Court, a formidable document with copies of all the records covering everything involved with *Roe v. Wade* from its inception. This collection became a small book printed as specified by the Court on pages measuring six by nine and a quarter inches. When finished in a rush by a New York printer acquainted with the Court's requirements, it came to 139 pages.

As Weddington tried to concentrate on the petitioner's brief, other demands kept distracting her. For example, Lucas recommended preparing another document not required by the Court, but one that everyone agreed was a good idea. This "supplementary appendix" amounted to a comprehensive textbook on all facets of the abortion issue—legal, medical, social, historical, and so on. It was put together with an impressive assemblage of articles, speeches, excerpts from books, and whatever else the justices and their staffs might find useful in preparing for *Roe v. Wade.*

Weddington's Texas case added pressure to an already pressurized institute staff as she frequently commandeered them to help, not always to Lucas's liking. The importance of her case also became apparent to proabortion leaders who offered to help her. One of them, Jimmye Kimmey, a political science teacher at Barnard College, had, for five years, been executive director of the New York–based Association for the Study of Abortion, an important informational source on the subject. Kimmey became an immense help to Weddington when she volunteered to select and organize *amici curiae.* (*Amicus curiae* means "friend of the court," someone who is not a party to a case but is allowed to file a brief that may help a court understand what is involved.) She had many contacts with people and organizations capable of offering, through amicus briefs, a wealth of information on the abortion issue, supplementing and strengthening the petitioner's brief. Before the August 17 deadline Kimmey had obtained forty-two such briefs signed by authorities from several fields of endeavor—scientific, medical, historical, social, religious, and legal—as well as leaders speaking for large numbers of American citizens.

One major brief, for example, became known as "the women's brief," for it was backed by seven major women's organizations, such as the American Association of University Women and the Young Women's Christian Association. The brief was also signed by a long list of well-known women, including writers, political leaders, lawyers, educators, and journalists.

One of the best-known lawyers associated with the birth-control movement, Harriet Pilpel, prepared a brief for the Planned Parenthood Federation of America and the American Association of Planned Parenthood Physicians. A well-known New York lawyer, Helen Buttenwieser, wrote a "religious brief" backed by a number of denominations, such as the American Friends Service Committee, the United Church of Christ, and the United Methodist Church. And the amicus briefs added numerous other perspectives on the abortion issue, such as those from medical and psychiatric organizations, including groups of practitioners independently formed to submit briefs. The legal profession was also represented by amicus briefs—for example, from the American Civil Liberties Union and a specially assembled group of women lawyers. When all Kimmey's amicus briefs were delivered, they provided the justices and their staffs with a voluminous amount of material relative to the complicated questions posed for the Court by *Roe v. Wade.*

As the summer went by, Sarah Weddington, beset by the crowded, frenetic atmosphere at the Madison Institute, found it more and more difficult to concentrate on the petitioner's brief that she knew was the most crucial of all the submissions to the Court. If a justice read nothing else pertaining to a case, to make a valid voting decision he would have to understand two key briefs, the petitioner's and the respondent's—each limited by Court rules to 150 pages. While Weddington had a certain amount of help from the institute staff and volunteers who increasingly recognized the importance of her case, it was never the intensive, experienced legal assistance she badly needed. But to her delight such help finally showed up in the middle of July, in the person of her husband.

Ron Weddington, whose work in Fort Worth had been completed, arrived in New York to visit his wife and was promptly enlisted to assist her on the brief. Together they reached out for help to many New York sources and to their friends in Austin who had access to the University of Texas law library. In New York, for example, they were helped by Alan Guttmacher, the leading doctor in the abortion law reform movement who had recently added his support to the repeal movement. The Weddingtons' friends in Austin frequently made library searches for court decisions Ron and Sarah wished to cite in the petitioner's brief. With hardly any time off, the Weddingtons devoted full days and much of their nights to researching and writing the brief until it was done.

When printed and ready for delivery, it was far more comprehensive than the comparable one filed with the three-judge court in Dallas. It covered the history of the case, beginning with Jane Roe's fruitless effort to obtain an abortion because of the Texas law. It went on to the three-judge court's decision, including its failure to order Henry Wade to stop enforcing the law, and finally, to Wade's announcement that he would continue prosecuting cases under the abortion law. The brief also covered the key medical facts involved with abortion. For instance, it stressed that contraception was not a fail-safe means of preventing pregnancy, leaving abortion the alternative in certain cases when a woman chose not to give birth. The document then turned to the key constitutional issue of personal privacy established by *Griswold v. Connecticut,* and the justices were invited to consider the constitutional amendments out of which this basic right was derived by *Griswold.*

The completed brief addressed a question being asked more and more by abortion opponents, one that would probably be raised before the Supreme Court by the state's attorneys: Is a fetus legally a person, with the rights of a person? The petitioner's brief answered no, stressing that the government had never considered the fetus a person. Laws against murder, for example, had never equated killing a fetus with homicide. The brief stated that homicide in Texas applied only to victims who had been born, and, in a footnote, indicated something that seemed to go without saying, that a fetus cannot be a United States citizen—citizens being defined by the Constitution's Fourteenth Amendment as "all persons born or naturalized in the United States . . ." And thus the argument continued to undermine the abortion opponents' contention that the surgical procedure amounted to homicide.

The petitioner's brief, printed in the Court's prescribed form, was filed in Washington prior to the deadline, and copies were mailed to the opposing lawyers in Texas. Meanwhile, Jay Floyd, the lawyer assigned to *Roe* by Henry Wade, had been unable to prepare the respondent's brief on time. He kept asking for and receiving extensions of the deadline, until the last, which the Clerk of the Supreme Court granted, emphasizing that the "final" deadline was a day in the middle of October. But even then, the respondent's brief arrived two or three days late.

Floyd's repeated delays did not result from his lack of interest in the case. On the contrary, following his argument before the three-judge court in Dallas, the lawyer became intensely interested in the abortion question, but while he was anxious to write the brief for the Supreme Court, some fifty other cases kept distracting him. Actually Floyd's interest had led him to become firmly opposed to abortion and convinced of the fetus's right to life. As he tried to make time for the *Roe* brief, he was contacted by three lawyers—one from Washington, two from Chicago—representing the National Right to Life Committee (founded by Dr. John C. Willke of Cincinnati). The two Chicago attorneys were preparing an amicus brief defending the Texas abortion law, and they offered to help Floyd with his respondent's brief. When his document was finally finished, Floyd began by discussing his personal conviction that the fetus is a human being whose right to life overrides the mother's right to privacy. Following his opening, a large percentage of the brief virtually duplicated material found in the amicus brief filed with the Court by the Chicago lawyers.

Despite this submission, Wade's side of the case had obviously failed to produce anything like the number of amicus briefs Jimmye Kimmey had rounded up for the opposing side. In the end very few amicus briefs were filed supporting the state. Besides the National Right to Life Committee, the friends of the Court included Mothers of the Unborn and an organization called LIFE (an acronym for League for Infants, Fetuses and the Elderly). The most powerful abortion opponent of all, the Catholic Church, was represented only by a state organization, the Association of Texas Diocesan Attorneys, whose amicus brief was prepared by a law professor.

When the Weddingtons returned from New York to Austin in late August, they hoped to establish their own law practice. But events involving *Roe v. Wade* continued to distract the couple, as well as Linda Coffee in Dallas. Until the middle of September their educated guesses told them they could win *Roe* with a vote of five justices to four, but suddenly Justice Black resigned on September 17, one week before his death, and Justice Harlan resigned on September 23 because of failing health. Now the guessing became much more complicated. If the hearing date for *Roe* were delayed until a full Court could hear the case, it might mean that President Nixon could, in the meantime, nominate two replacement justices who would undoubtedly be conservatives opposed to abortion. Should that happen, the educated guesses said *Roe* could lose by five to four. But then if the president took his time, as he had in the past, *Roe* might be decided by the remaining seven justices—in which case it would be a good guess to say it would win by four to three. Coffee, Weddington, and their fellow abortion proponents now could only hope the Court would hear *Roe* as soon as possible with the seven-member Court. The opposing attorneys hoped for the opposite to happen, and they began thinking of how they might delay the proceedings until the president's nominations were confirmed.

As they waited that fall, Coffee and Weddington were plagued by Roy Lucas's insistence that he should argue *Roe* before the Court. Indeed, without telling Weddington, he wrote to the Court and announced that he would be arguing *Roe.* When Coffee and Weddington learned of this they were upset; however, Weddington offered to compromise and share the time before the Court, if Lucas had to appear. Lucas then claimed he was best qualified to do the job, having had a lot of experience with the Court whereas Weddington had had none. But his insistence encountered a lot of disagreement, mostly from women who firmly believed that *Roe* should be argued by a woman. The extent and value of his experience with the Court were also questioned. Lucas had numerous enemies among abortion proponents, and upon learning of what he was up to, some loudly disputed his contention that he could do better than Weddington. When finally Lucas claimed he had earned the right to argue the case, it was too much for Weddington. The case had never been for sale, she said. Her predominant right to argue the case became clear when she and Coffee learned that the justices favored hearing attorneys representing the principals in cases before the Court. Lucas obviously didn't qualify. When the oral arguments were finally set for December 13, the Clerk of the Court demanded to know who would appear for Jane Roe. Coffee wrote to him stating that Jane Roe had been Coffee and Weddington's client, and Weddington would argue the case. That settled the dispute with Lucas. Weddington finally knew she would soon appear before the nation's highest court.

Her preparations for the encounter included, among other efforts, a number of informal "moot courts" (make-believe courts—in this instance mimicking the Supreme Court). Weddington played herself in the upcoming oral arguments while the justices' roles were played by University of Texas Law School professors and students, as well as friends acquainted with the pros and cons of the abortion issue. Weddington tried out remarks she might use in the half hour she would have before the Court, and those playing the justices questioned her as members of the Court might on December 13. The moot courts were extremely helpful as testing grounds for her presentation before the real Court and for considering a wide variety of questions the real justices might ask her. Just prior to the hearing date at the Court a very important, more formal moot court was held in Washington for Weddington by some of the country's most informed proabortion authorities. By the time all the make-believe justices had finished with her, she had been exposed to and learned the answers for just about every conceivable question that might be thrown at her by Chief Justice Burger and his brethren.

On October 21, everyone hoping for a *Roe* victory listened with trepidation as President Nixon announced in a nationwide television broadcast his two nominations to fill the Harlan and Black vacancies on the Supreme Court. The nominees were sixty-four-year-old Lewis F. Powell of Virginia, a former president of the American Bar Association, and forty-seven-year-old William H. Rehnquist of Arizona, who twenty years earlier had served as a law clerk for Justice Robert H. Jackson. Powell was a political moderate, while Rehnquist was known as an extreme conservative. How Powell would vote in the abortion case was difficult to predict, but Rehnquist's vote would, without doubt, come down in favor of Henry Wade. Now the question was how long it would take for the Senate to confirm (or reject) the two men.

On November 15, the day when the *Roe* hearing date was finally set for December 13, the Senate's vote on the two nominations was still weeks away, probably nip and tuck with the scheduled hearing. But then on November 30, Henry Wade's counsel, Jay Floyd, filed a formal motion with the Supreme Court requesting postponement of the *Roe v. Wade* oral arguments until the two new members of the Court were confirmed and seated, in order to allow a full, nine-member Court to consider the case. For one week the Court remained silent on Floyd's motion, leaving the proabortion people fearing that the postponement would be approved and their chances of winning would vanish. Meanwhile, on December 6, the Senate confirmed Lewis Powell's nomination by a vote of eighty-nine to one but continued consideration of William Rehnquist's nomination. The next day, December 7, the Court denied Floyd's motion, thus assuring that in six days the seven-member Court would hear *Roe v. Wade.*

Coffee, Weddington, and their friends relaxed, returning to their educated guess that predicted they had a good chance of winning with a four-to-three vote, based primarily on how Justices Brennan, Douglas, and White had voted favoring *Griswold v. Connecticut.*

12

Argued and Argued Again

At 9:45 A.M. on December 13, 1971, the courtroom of the Supreme Court of the United States was rapidly filling with a capacity crowd, which indicated that the oral arguments for an important case were to be heard at 10:00. The three hundred or so seats in the elegant courtroom, the size of a small theater or church, were divided into sections for the people arriving to witness the proceedings. The sections included 85 seats for the press, a 170-seat section for visiting lawyers, a 30-seat "VIP" section for guests invited by the justices, and two small sections reserved for guests and associates of the opposing lawyers appearing before the Court. The greatest number of seats were kept for lucky members of the public allowed into the courtroom from a first-come, first-served waiting line outside. Finally, a small number of seats, a "three-minute section," accommodated groups, mostly tourists, who were allowed, one after another, to enter the courtroom quietly and remain for only three minutes—the in-and-out flow continuing all during the oral arguments. The spectators that morning became the privileged few to witness the single Supreme Court decision-making proceeding open to the press and public; all the others are strictly private.

The privileged few—whether there for the first or the hundredth time—couldn't help but sense the awe inspired by the magnificent room, measuring eighty-two by ninety-one feet. Here, at the heart of the great marble palace, the walls were paneled with "Ivory Vein" marble from Spain. The paneling was set off by twenty-four massive columns of delicately tinted marble from the famous Montarrenti quarry in Italy. The columns rising forty-four feet supported the ornate ceiling decorated in striking reds and blues with gold gilt. All this was set off by heavy red drapes and the dark luster of solid Honduran mahogany. At the front of the room stood the long bench where many of the nation's most controversial issues come for a final settlement. Behind and projecting above the bench, the audience saw the backs of nine chairs, all different, each having been selected by and designed for the justice it would seat. The courtroom clock, suspended above and to the rear of the center chair where the chief justice sits, was approaching 10:00 A.M. And in a "robing room" behind the heavy drapes below the clock, the seven justices—two fewer than the full membership of nine—were donning their black robes, getting ready for the oral arguments to begin in a few minutes.

As the audience settled down, they saw in front of the bench the counsels representing both sides of the cases to be argued. Some of the lawyers were seated, others standing, around two mahogany tables separated by a podium only a few feet in front of where the chief justice would sit. With one exception, they were from Texas and Georgia, the states where the two cases to be argued originated. One was the "counsel for petitioner," Sarah Weddington, who would argue the first case to be heard. She was accompanied by Linda Coffee and the New York lawyer, Roy Lucas. At the table on the opposite side of the podium sat the "counsel for respondent," Jay Floyd. He would argue in opposition to Sarah Weddington—as he had done in the three-judge court in Dallas. Floyd was accompanied by an associate from Henry Wade's staff. The lawyers who would argue the Georgia case were seated in chairs right behind the two counsel tables.

In the moments before 10:00 Weddington glanced around the nearby reserved sections and was greeted with smiles and nods from numerous friends and supporters—like Jimmye Kimmey, who had worked so hard on the amicus briefs; two young men who had helped Weddington through the difficult summer at the Madison Institute; Harriet Pilpel, counsel for the Planned Parenthood Federation of America; several friends and teachers who had come from Texas to see her argue before the High Court; and her husband, Ron, sitting in the lawyers' section. Sarah Weddington knew that one lawyer in that section did not wish her well: one of the two from Chicago who had helped Floyd prepare the Texas brief. She had met him on some other occasion, and as both entered the Court that morning, they had said hello. However, he had added, "It will be a sad day for the country if you win today. I am counting on your losing."

Two important persons were not there: the actual petitioner, the anonymous Jane Roe, and the actual respondent, the real Henry Wade. Despite their absence, their names would identify one of the most famous—or infamous—decisions in the history of the Court: *Roe v. Wade.*

As the minute hand on the Court's clock came near to marking the hour, a hush fell over the audience in anticipation of the exact moment of 10:00. In the robing room the seven justices shook hands with one another, engaging in a custom introduced around the turn of the century by Chief Justice Melville Fuller. It signified, in his words, that "harmony of aims if not of views is the Court's guiding principle." The justices then lined up, and at precisely 10:00, signaled by the Marshal of the Court banging his gavel, the drapes were parted, the justices walked out, and they proceeded to their seats. As they did so, the marshal announced, "The Honorable, the chief justice and the associate justices of the Supreme Court of the United States"—hesitating a moment as everyone in the room stood up, then continuing—"Oyez, oyez, oyez! All persons having business before the Honorable, the Supreme Court of the United States, are admonished to draw near and give their attention, for the Court is now sitting. God save the United States and this Honorable Court!" The justices sat down; the marshal banged his gavel, and everyone else in the room sat down.

In the next few minutes several young, neatly dressed pages appeared and placed briefs and other papers before the justices. Then in a brief ceremony in front of the justices, two attorneys who had been approved to practice before the Court were formally admitted to the Supreme Court bar. They pledged—"I will demean myself, as an attorney and counselor of this court, uprightly and according to law. . . ."—each placing his hand on a Bible that had been used by clerks of the Court since 1808. Meanwhile, Sarah Weddington became more and more nervous, acutely aware that she was about to appear for only the second time in her life in a contested case before a court. Glancing again at the instructions provided by the Court, she hastily reviewed for the umpteenth time what she was supposed to do next: "When counsel's turn comes for argument," it said, "he will proceed to the rostrum without being called. He should not begin until he has been recognized by the Chief Justice. . . ." She had previously found the two sentences irksome—three "he's"—but no time to think about that now . . . the chief justice was speaking.

"We'll hear arguments in Number eighteen, *Roe against Wade,*" he announced, and according to the instructions, Sarah Weddington stood up and stepped to the podium. Many of the spectators, not acquainted with the case and expecting a "he" to stand up, were surprised that a "she" went to the podium. More than one onlooker had assumed she was someone's secretary. But there she was: a young, attractive woman, five feet, seven inches tall, with strawberry-blond hair falling over her shoulders—and about to argue before the awesome Court led by the imposing Warren E. Burger.

"Mrs. Weddington," the chief justice said, "you may proceed whenever you are ready."

Weddington was nervous, very nervous, but she was ready because she had come to the Supreme Court steeped in her subject—and this helped allay her nervousness. She was prepared to speak extemporaneously for most of her allotted thirty minutes, or any part of the time when not responding to the justices' questions. She knew that the Court's oral arguments are mainly for the justices to ask questions, not simply to sit quietly and listen to counsels' speeches. Moreover, by this time, the justices had been buried in—one said "overwhelmed by"—everything they might ever need to know about every facet—legal, medical, religious, and so on and so forth—of the abortion subject. Piled one on top of the other, the pages of the briefs filed to enlighten the justices and their staffs were the equivalent of a book more than one foot thick—and they had arrived with heaps of other material sent to the Court, like the five-hundred-plus pages of the supplementary index devised by Roy Lucas. But a short period of silence that followed the chief justice's invitation to proceed demanded that Weddington provide still more on the subject, and she complied:

"Mr. Chief Justice, and may it please the Court." She spoke according to protocol, then began a quick review of the facts of her case. "Certainly Jane Roe brought her suit as soon as she knew she was pregnant. As soon as she had sought an abortion and been denied, she came to federal court. She came on behalf of a class of women, and I don't think there's any question but what women in Texas continue to desire abortions and to seek them out, outside of our state . . ."

"Mrs. Weddington!"—the first interruption came from the man who had just asked her to proceed, the chief justice, and he wanted to know something about *Vuitch,* exactly the kind of abrupt subject change Weddington had been taught to expect and deal with during the recent moot courts held for her benefit. He wondered if *Vuitch*—the decision involving the Washington, D.C., doctor—had already settled some of the issues brought to the Court by *Roe.* She contended that the issues settled by *Vuitch* were not relevant to *Roe,* and that satisfied the chief justice. Weddington returned to what she was prepared to say, but more interruptions with questions took her away from it. She provided the answers, but soon began to worry that her thirty minutes were rapidly dwindling, and she might lose the chance to press a point with the seven men at the bench concerning something they could never experience, pregnancy.

"I think it's without question," she stated when the chance came, "that pregnancy to a woman can completely disrupt her life. It disrupts her body, it disrupts her education, it disrupts her employment, and it often disrupts her entire family life. And we feel that because of the impact on the woman, this certainly, insofar as there are any rights which are fundamental, is a matter which is of such fundamental and basic concern to the woman involved that she should be allowed to make the choice as to whether to continue or to terminate her pregnancy."

"Mrs. Weddington!" one of the justices interrupted, causing her to wonder if he had been listening. She wasn't sure who he was, but a "cheat sheet" on the podium, identifying each justice by where he sat, told her he was Potter Stewart. Here was one of the two dissenters in *Griswold v. Connecticut,* who might very well oppose *Roe.* Of all the justices along the bench before her, Weddington would have preferred hearing from Douglas, who wrote the *Griswold* majority decision, the justice most responsible for the constitutional protection of personal privacy. But Justice Douglas—the Court's most senior member with thirty-two years' service—paid little attention to her. In fact, he occupied himself busily writing something with a pen or pencil—and he continued doing so all during her half hour. (Those who knew him didn't find this unusual. He seldom asked questions during oral arguments and frequently spent the time writing.)

"Mrs. Weddington," Justice Stewart said, "so far . . . you've told us about the important impact of this [Texas] law and made a very eloquent policy argument against it. I trust you are going to get to what provisions of the Constitution you rely on. Because, of course . . . we cannot here be involved simply with matters of policy, as you know."

Weddington was ready for the question and reminded the justice that the three-judge court in Texas "held that the right to determine whether or not to continue a pregnancy rested upon the Ninth Amendment. . . ." and "I do feel that . . . is an appropriate place for the freedom to rest." But then she went on to say she felt the "Fourteenth Amendment is equally an appropriate place, under the rights of persons to life, liberty, and the pursuit of happiness."

The justice then asked, "You're relying in this branch of your argument [today] simply on the due process clause of the Fourteenth Amendment?"

Weddington replied that originally they [she and Linda Coffee] had brought their case including the Fourteenth's due process and equal protection clauses, as well as the Ninth Amendment and "a variety" of other constitutional amendments.

"And," the justice added with a good-natured barb, "anything else that might obtain?"

"Yeah, right!" Weddington replied, almost forgetting where she was and prompting laughter from the audience. Then quickly getting back to the seriousness of the occasion, she said, "One of the purposes of the Constitution was to guarantee to individuals the right to determine the course of their own lives." And later she supported this by claiming that the liberty of personal privacy came from various parts of the Constitution. She cited the Court's *Griswold* decision where

Justice Douglas referred to a "penumbra" of rights involved with the entire purpose of the Constitution, and she concluded that one of these rights guaranteed individuals the right to determine the course of their own lives.

Much of Weddington's remaining time was taken by Justice Stewart joined by Justice White. They were particularly interested in her views on the timing of an abortion during the course of a given pregnancy. She had felt that the question of timing was not a matter before the Court in *Roe v. Wade,* but she found that it was of considerable interest to the two justices. Justice White asked if she meant that a woman should have the right to an abortion at any time during a pregnancy up to the point of birth.

"It is our position," Weddington replied, "that the freedom involved is that of a woman to determine whether or not to continue a pregnancy. Obviously, I have a much more difficult time saying that the state has no interest in a late pregnancy."

"Why?" the justice asked. "Why is that?"

"I think it is more the emotional response to a late pregnancy," Weddington answered, "rather than [a constitutional question]."

The questions shifted to another subject: Why was the Texas law passed? Weddington said no legislative history had been found to help answer the question. However, she noted that court cases dealing with the law indicated that the crime was committed by the person (usually the doctor) performing an abortion, except when it was necessary to save the mother's life. The female involved remained guiltless.

"In Texas, the woman is the victim," Weddington explained. "The state cannot deny the effects that this law has on the women of Texas. Certainly there are problems regarding even the use of contraception. Abortion now for a woman is safer than childbirth. In the absence of abortion, or legal, medically safe abortions, women often resort to the illegal abortion, which certainly carries risks of death, all the side effects such as severe infection, permanent sterility, all the complications that result. And in fact, if the woman is unable to get either a legal abortion or an illegal abortion in our state, she can do a self-abortion, which is certainly . . . by far the most dangerous. And that is no crime."

This discourse led to another line of questioning concerning how the Texas case law viewed the aborted fetus. Weddington pointed out that the state had never considered a fetus as a person, with the legal rights of a person. The doctor terminating the development of a fetus by abortion was not prosecuted or penalized as a murderer. And the aborted fetus was not subject to the legalities of a dead person—no requirements for a death certificate, for example.

Weddington found it difficult to understand how her impromptu replies to random questions would, for better or worse, influence the Court's decision-making process. Years later she recalled, "I had been concentrating so hard during the thirty minutes I stood before the Court that afterwards I could remember only a little of what had been said." Her husband and Linda Coffee helped her recall the questions and her answers, but she still wanted to hear herself on the tape made by the Court of the oral arguments—but she had to wait three years for it to be released by the National Archives. Regardless of her concerns, her listeners generally agreed she had given a smooth, articulate performance.

Its end was signaled by a red light on the podium causing Chief Justice Burger to say, "Thank you, Mrs. Weddington." He then turned toward the opposing attorney and simply said, "Mr. Floyd." Sarah sat down, and Jay Floyd stepped to the podium. He had come with a carefully prepared outline of what he hoped to cover, but he immediately made a blunder that tainted his entire performance.

"Mr. Chief Justice, may it please the Court," he said, then startled the chief and his associate justices by saying, "It's an old joke, but when a man argues against two beautiful ladies like this, they're going to have the last word." The complete silence from the bench and throughout the room flustered the counsel. Warren Burger's fury over the inappropriate comment was obvious, and it discombobulated the Texas lawyer's precious half hour before the Court.

Finally breaking the silence, Floyd began his argument contending that *Roe v. Wade* had become a moot case once Jane Roe's pregnancy ended with the birth of her child. His opponents listened in disbelief. Didn't he know *Roe* was a class action? If he didn't know, Justice Stewart immediately informed him of the fact, noting that since it was a class action the Court's consideration of *Roe* could continue with assurance "that there are at any given time unmarried pregnant females in Texas."

Nevertheless, Floyd continued to pursue his mootness argument, but he was brought up short by a question from Justice Stewart, who asked, "What procedure would you suggest for *any* pregnant female in the state of Texas ever to get any judicial consideration of this constitutional claim [being considered in the case at hand]?"

"Your Honor . . . I do not believe it can be done. . . . I think she makes her choice prior to the time she becomes pregnant. That is the time of choice. . . . I think pregnancy may terminate that choice. That's when."

"Maybe she makes her choice when she decides to live in Texas," Justice Stewart said—and the laughter Floyd had been denied with his "old joke" spread through the courtroom.

"May I proceed?" the lawyer asked as the room quieted down.

But the justice had one more remark for him: "There's no restriction on moving, you know," he added, prompting another round of laughter.

Justice Thurgood Marshall joined Justice Stewart in trying to learn from Floyd why Texas kept the nineteenth-century abortion law on its books. What were the state's interests? one of the justices asked. Floyd had no clear answer. He said it was really something for the state legislature to decide, not the Court. He was told that in a constitutional case like *Roe* it was important for the Court to know what interest the state had in the law. The lawyer then expressed his personal opinion on the matter and said, "I would think that even when this statute was first passed, there was some concern for the unborn fetus." As for the state's present concern for the fetus, Floyd added, "We say there is life from the moment of impregnation [in the sexual act]."

"And do you have any scientific evidence to support that?" Justice Marshall asked.

Floyd referred to his respondent's brief for an answer, and said, "Well, we begin . . . in our brief with the development of the human embryo, carrying it through the development of the fetus from about seven to nine days after conception."

"Well, what about six days?" Justice Marshall asked.

"We don't know."

"Well this statute goes all the way back to one hour."

"Mr. Justice," the lawyer pleaded, "there are unanswerable questions in this field." Now Floyd prompted laughter in the audience.

"I appreciate it," the justice said.

"This is an artless statement on my part," Floyd confessed.

"I withdraw the question," the justice said.

"Thank you," said Floyd, but he added one more confused remark, saying, "Or when does the soul come into the unborn, if a person believes in a soul? I don't know."

Floyd then went back to his contention that *Roe v. Wade* was not for the High Court to decide. He said, "We think these matters are matters of policy, which should be properly addressed by the state legislature."

His time before the Court ended with another question from Justice Stewart. He pointed out that the Texas abortion law had no exception for women who have been raped, then asked, "Such a woman wouldn't have had a choice [to obtain a legal abortion], would she?" The lawyer's attempt to deal with that point was terminated by the red light on the podium and a thank you from the chief justice.

During a brief pause in the proceedings the lawyers arguing the Texas case were replaced by the two with the Georgia case, *Doe v. Bolton.* Margie Hames, counsel for the petitioner, argued that Georgia's abortion reform law had created so many "cumbersome, costly and time-consuming" procedures they virtually ruled out the right to terminate a pregnancy. Dorothy Beasley, the counsel for the respondent (Bolton), argued that the Georgia law was concerned with the value of fetal life, which the state recognized as another "human entity" that should be recognized by the abortion law. Observers of the day's oral arguments gave Beasley the highest grade of the four counsels for her clear, articulate presentation of the Georgia case. Sarah Weddington was second best. Incidentally, Beasley had been scheduled to return to the Court in thirty-five days to argue for the state in *Furman v. Georgia,* a landmark case on the death penalty. While she argued for life in *Doe v. Bolton,* she would argue for death in *Furman*—and would lose in both cases.

When the oral arguments were finished, the lawyers involved met outside the courtroom with their associates and friends to assess how the seven justices might vote. Anyone's guess was as good as the next person's, and the guessing game went on for one year, one month, and ten days. The conjecturing was swayed by occasional rumors seeping out of the marble palace, but no one really had any idea of what transpired in the privacy of the Court's inner chambers. The only public utterance came in late June 1972, not to announce the expected decision but simply to issue a simple, yet very surprising notice: The abortion cases were to be reargued in the fall. This was highly unusual because cases were ordinarily reargued only to go over a specific point. But the notice said nothing of the kind. It only noted that Justice Douglas had filed a dissent against reargument.

Of course, the news intensified speculation about *Roe*'s fate. The most widely accepted guess said the rearguments had been scheduled so the two new justices, William Rehnquist and Lewis Powell, could vote on the decision. Whatever the reason, the addition of two Nixon appointees to the bench worried those who favored *Roe v. Wade.*

Three weeks prior to the reargument notice, Sarah Weddington had become a candidate for a seat in the Texas legislature and planned to spend all her time campaigning before election day, November 7. Now she had to take time to work with Linda Coffee and prepare for the rearguments. This included researching and writing a seventeen-page supplementary petitioner's brief required by the Court. And again Weddington had to devote a lot of time to doing homework for her second round with the justices. The date was finally set for mid-October, her most important month for campaigning. She and her husband, Ron, drove to Washington a few days early to participate in moot courts organized for her and Margie Hames by several leaders of the proabortion movement. The importance of all the preparation was emphasized when Weddington learned she would be facing a new and probably more formidable opponent. Henry Wade had replaced Jay Floyd with Robert C. Flowers, a Texas assistant attorney general.

The rearguments duplicated the earlier arguments in a number of ways, except the justices focused more on questions about the development of, and the life and death of, the fetus in respect to abortion. They wanted to hear more from the *Roe v. Wade* counsels as to when a fetus legally became a person protected by the Constitution.

Weddington stood firmly by her assertion that a fetus, until birth, is not legally a person, and that position remained essential to her case. This became clear when Justice Stewart asked her, "If it were established that an unborn fetus is a person, within the protection of the Fourteenth Amendment, you would have almost an impossible case here, would you not?" And she replied, "I would have a very difficult case." However, she emphasized that the Texas law did not pose that difficulty, because it made no claim that a fetus is a person.

Robert Flowers interpreted the law otherwise. In his turn at the podium he immediately said, "It is impossible for me to trace, within my allotted time, the development of the fetus from the date of conception to the date of birth. But it is the position of the state of Texas that upon conception we have a human being, a person within the concept of the Constitution of the United States and that of Texas also."

Flowers's firm stance opened him up to a grilling for most of his time, with the justices wanting to know how the state had arrived at its position. "Now how should that question [you raise about the fetus] be decided?" Justice Blackmun asked Flowers. "Is it a legal question, a constitutional question, a medical question, a philosophical question, a religious question, or what?"

Obviously the lawyer didn't know. "Your Honor," he replied, "we feel that it could be decided by a legislature . . . that can bring before it the medical testimony, the actual people who do the research. . . ."

"You think it's basically a medical question?"

"From a constitutional standpoint, no sir," Flowers answered, then admitted the question rested "fairly and squarely before the Court." And he added sympathetically, "We don't envy the Court for having to make this decision."

At one point during Weddington's turn, Justice Blackmun asked an interesting question relevant to the fetus's being or not being a person. He noted that the Court, having just recently decided *Furman v. Georgia,* had ruled the death penalty unconstitutional. He asked if she found this inconsistent with her support of abortion. She answered no, pointing out what she had stated before, that illegal abortions had never been punished as homicides because the fetus had not legally been considered a person—as was the murder victim in *Furman.*

When Flowers's time was up, Weddington used a few minutes she had saved from her half hour for a rebuttal, and at that point she talked to the nine men about the decisions that they, along with pregnant women, faced.

"No one is more keenly aware of the gravity of the issues or the moral implications of this case," she said, speaking of herself. "But it is a case that must be decided on the Constitution. . . . We are not here to advocate abortion. We do not ask the Court to rule that abortion is good or desirable in any particular situation. We *are* here to advocate that the decision as to whether or not a particular woman will continue to carry or will terminate a pregnancy is a decision that should be made by that individual. That in fact she has a constitutional right to make that decision for herself, and that the state has shown no interest in interfering with that decision."

When she finished, Chief Justice Burger said, "Thank you, Mrs. Weddington; thank you, Mr. Flowers. The case is submitted."

The rearguments of the Georgia case followed, with Margie Hames and her opponent, Dorothy Beasley, covering pretty much the same questions argued before. When they were finished, both abortion cases were finally on the way to decisions.

Upon leaving the Court, Sarah Weddington and Linda Coffee, joined by several other persons who favored *Roe,* felt the justices had already made up their minds before rehearing the arguments. But how? That remained impossible to answer for more than a year. The making up of the justices' minds depended on numerous secret meetings held from right after the original oral arguments through the rearguments and on to the decision day. The inviolate secrecy of those gatherings was insured by a unique, beautifully appointed room in the marble palace.

13

Absolutely Secret

The conference room of the Supreme Court of the United States is one of the nation's most secluded meeting rooms. It is reserved for the country's nine highest judges to confer in secret, usually on Fridays during the Court's term from October into the following June or July. Here, with only the justices present, they meet with the assurance that the room's privacy is absolute. If someone outside must communicate with those inside, it is done through written messages received at the door by the junior associate justice (the latest appointed to the Court). This zealously guarded privacy provides a precious opportunity for the justices to work alone, removed as much as possible from public emotions and prejudices that could distract them from their essential role of interpreting how the Constitution of the United States applies to the cases they decide. Even the justices themselves cannot be sure of how a given case will be decided until they discuss their voting intentions as they meet in secret in the conference room.

The chamber is a beautiful, wood-paneled room, and from its high ceiling there hangs a large, elegant chandelier intricately trimmed with scores of sparkling glass beads. It is suspended over an extra-large conference table surrounded by nine chairs with high backs. The chief justice sits at one end of the long table, and the senior associate justice sits facing him at the other end. Four seats to the chief's left and three to his right accommodate the seven other associate justices. Behind the senior associate justice stands a fireplace with a clock on the mantel. And on the wall above there's a portrait of John Marshall, the fourth chief justice of the Court. Marshall served from 1801 to 1835 and won the acclaim of historians for raising the prestige and power of the great institution.

In this conference room, since the building was new in the 1930s, nine justices have made some of the most important decisions in the Court's history. On December 16, 1971, they were gathered there, seven justices in number, to take up *Roe v. Wade,* argued three days earlier with its companion case, *Doe v. Bolton.* Warren Burger took his place in the chief justice's chair at the head of the table, and William Douglas sat in the senior associate justice's chair at the opposite end of the table. Seats at the sides of the table were occupied by the five other justices, Byron White, Potter Stewart, William Brennan, Thurgood Marshall, and Harry Blackmun. Although the justices had yet to decide which abortion case would be the lead case, the chief justice began the meeting with *Roe v. Wade.* He started by expressing how he felt about the case, then, beginning with Justice Douglas, he went around the table giving each man an opportunity to express how he reacted to *Roe* and how he expected to vote, if he knew at that point. The same procedure was followed with *Doe v. Bolton* until all the justices had discussed the Georgia case and how the voting might go.

The justices who kept tallies of the possible votes concluded that potentially a majority of five would affirm (agree with) the *Roe v. Wade* decision delivered by the three-judge panel in Dallas. The five included four justices from the Warren Court—Douglas, Brennan, Stewart, and Marshall—plus one Nixon appointee, Blackmun. If the majority held together, it was probable Jane Roe would win, either by a vote of six to one, or five to two. Justice White would definitely vote to reverse (reject) the Texas decision. The chief justice, however, was ambivalent, so his vote might go one way or the other. Tallies of possible votes for *Doe v. Bolton* indicated less than a majority would affirm the Georgia panel's decision. Only three would vote to affirm, while two, the chief justice and Justice White, would vote to reverse the lower-court decision. The remaining two justices, Douglas and Blackmun, were undecided, feeling the case might be remanded (sent back to the lower court) for clarification of the case record.

The biggest surprise at the conference was that Justice Blackmun joined and thus completed a majority of five who expected to affirm *Roe v. Wade.* He was the junior justice of the seven present, having served only one full term on the Court. The kind of voting record he would establish was still unclear, although it seemed safe to say it would be a conservative one following the lead of the new chief justice—and the philosophy of the president who had appointed them. The media, assuming Harry Blackmun would mimic Warren Burger's conservatism, had nicknamed them the "Minnesota Twins"—a tag Blackmun disliked. When it came to abortion, which President Nixon vehemently opposed, it was hard to imagine his ire should one or both of his first two successful appointees to the Court turn out to be proabortion. But here in the privacy of the conference room it appeared to be happening, to the surprise of the four Warren Court justices with whom Blackmum was joining to affirm a proabortion case. What's more, Warren Burger wasn't sure which way to go.

A still bigger surprise was waiting for Justice Douglas back in his chambers after the conference. When he told his law clerks about Justice Blackmun's unexpected revelation, they were not surprised. Not only had they heard about Blackmun's intentions from his clerks, but they had also learned that he would like to write the majority opinion for *Roe v. Wade.* Justice Douglas's clerks told this to their boss, knowing he could grant Blackmun his wish. According to the Court's protocol the senior justice of a voting majority, Douglas in this case, had the responsibility for choosing who would write the majority opinion, and he could choose Blackmun.

Actually, this had occurred to Douglas at the conference. That afternoon he quickly conferred with the other three justices of the *Roe* majority and they, too, favored assigning Blackmun the opinion. They liked the idea, for they agreed that Blackmun's careful, meticulous manner of going about things and his medical-legal background at the Mayo Clinic made him a good choice to write the difficult opinion that *Roe* required.

(Here is what his assignment entailed: In conference the majority of five justices indicated their intentions to vote for the *Roe* decision. But the question still remained, "What precisely would the decision say?" Blackmun would face the challenge of putting the answer into writing to the satisfaction of all five in the majority, himself included. It would require writing and rewriting draft after draft of the opinion until one version finally met the approval of the full majority. The resulting "majority opinion" would then become the key document of the whole affair, for it would state for posterity what the Court's decision titled *Roe v. Wade* was all about.)

But before Douglas could make the Blackmun assignment, he had another surprise, an unhappy one, when he received the chief justice's list of opinion assignments for current cases. There Burger had on his own assigned Blackmun both the *Roe v. Wade* and *Doe v. Bolton* majority opinions. Douglas was furious that his prerogative to make the assignment had been violated. Furthermore, Blackmun had not favored affirming the Georgia case.

Justice Blackmun was also concerned about the dual assignment. As one of the *Roe* majority of five, he wanted to draft that opinion, but he was unhappy about the confusing assignment to do the same for the Georgia case. However, he agreed to give it a try.

Meanwhile, in a memorandum to the chief justice, Douglas expressed his dismay over what had happened. In reply, Burger explained that in the conference he found a lot of confusion as to what the justices would be approving or disapproving when they had to vote on the abortion cases. He had decided the confusion might be cleared up in the process of drafting the opinions. He felt Blackmun would be especially adept at this.

Five months later, on May 18, 1972, Blackmun circulated his "first and tentative draft" for the *Roe v. Wade* opinion. But after their long wait, his brethren of the *Roe* majority found the seventeen-page draft most disappointing. In a covering memo with the draft, the author explained that the complicated, sensitive issues made it difficult to write an opinion that could retain majority support. His solution, as the draft revealed, was to narrow down the opinion to a single issue that he felt could command a majority. For that he chose the now well-known route of declaring the Texas abortion law unconstitutionally vague—which it certainly was. This, Blackmun felt, would allow the Court to dispose of *Roe v. Wade* without becoming needlessly mired in its complexities.

In the memo's final paragraph, Blackmun said he found the Georgia case even more complex and was "tentatively of the view" that it should be held over to the Court's next term, when it could be reargued before a full bench of nine justices. He added that his draft for a *Doe* opinion would be ready soon, and it might help resolve the question of reargument.

The opinion and covering memo distressed Justice Douglas and his three brethren of the *Roe* majority. They had two concerns about what Blackmun offered.

The first was immediately raised by Justice William Brennan in a letter to Blackmun. He complained that the draft overlooked the "core constitutional question" the majority of five had hoped to pursue. This would have *Roe* declare state laws unconstitutional if they made abortion illegal during the "trimester" (three months) immediately following conception and before viability of the fetus (when it could first survive on its own). Brennan stressed that, according to his conference notes, the majority of five (including Blackmun) felt this was the ultimate question the Court had to face on the abortion issue. It had to be dealt with if a woman's personal privacy—as recently established by *Griswold v. Connecticut*—was to apply to abortion as well as birth control. *Roe v. Wade,* Brennan proposed, offered an opportunity for the Court to face up to the issue. But doing so, he and his colleagues understood, could be an extraordinary move forcing most of the states to rewrite their laws in ways that would legalize abortion. This could expose the justices to accusations of misusing their judicial powers by acting as superlegislators. On the other hand, to dispose of *Roe* on the vagueness issue could be criticized as a retreat from a difficult constitutional question that would have to be faced sooner or later.

The second concern was triggered by Blackmun's "tentative view" that the Georgia case should be reargued in the next term. Any mention of reargument incensed Justice Douglas who feared it could serve as an excuse for the chief justice to move to have both abortion cases reargued. Douglas became almost conspiratorial over this concern. He suspected Burger of plotting to bring the two latest Nixon appointees into the cases in order to help defeat them. He assumed that Justices Powell and Rehnquist would join Burger and White to reverse *Roe* and *Doe*. They would then need only one more vote to kill the abortion issue, possibly for a long time. Douglas then worried that the one vote needed for reargument might come from Blackmun.

In the last weeks of the 1972 term Justice Douglas's efforts to make sure the abortion cases were decided that term caused a great deal of extra tension at the Court in the tensest days of the year. He urged Blackmun to continue working on the Texas and Georgia opinions so, one way or another, both could be affirmed in that term. Meanwhile he opposed any move to have them reargued in the 1973 term. There was no point in delaying them, he maintained, saying they had been "as thoroughly worked over and considered as any cases ever before the Court in my time."

Although he was supported by his three brethren from the Warren Court, Douglas faced a losing battle. Suddenly the chief justice circulated a memo that brought the situation to a head. "I have had a great many problems," he wrote, "with these [abortion] cases from the outset. They are not as simple for me as they appear to be for others. . . . This is as sensitive and difficult an issue as any in this Court in my time and I want to hear more and think more when I am not trying to sort out several dozen other difficult cases.

"Hence, I vote to reargue early in the next term."

Douglas, in a swift note to Burger, expressed his fury and threatened to go public with what was happening if the Court voted to reargue. He implied that the chief justice was manipulating the Court to increase the chances of killing the abortion cases. Nevertheless, the Court voted in favor of rearguing, and Harry Blackmun's vote was the one that did it. The brief announcement of the delay, simply noting that Douglas had dissented, was the only official word of what had happened. The wrangle involved was hidden by the Court's inviolate secrecy—or supposedly so. But on the fourth of July, 1972, five days after the term had ended, a front-page, unsigned article in the *Washington Post* told about the Douglas–Burger disagreements under a headline stating MOVE BY BURGER MAY SHIFT COURT'S STAND ON ABORTION. The chief justice, a stickler for preserving the Court's rigid secrecy, was furious. He understandably assumed the story had come from Douglas, who, from his vacation home in Washington State, strenuously denied it in a letter to Burger.

As the next several months would confirm, Justice Douglas's assumptions were largely wrong. For example, he apparently overlooked one reason that possibly weighed heavily in

Burger's desire to delay the abortion cases until the Court's 1973 term. At the time, near the end of the 1972 term, the Court was on the verge of handing down another bombshell of a case, *Furman v. Georgia,* declaring the death penalty unconstitutional (and it did so on June 29, the last day of the term, with a five-to-four decision). For the relatively new Burger Court, this highly controversial decision seemed enough for one term without another, even more explosive, decision legalizing abortion. Regardless of what contributed to the reargument vote, the rejection of Justice Douglas's pressures undoubtedly led to a much more powerful *Roe v. Wade* in the 1973 term compared to what the 1972 term might have produced.

The difference was made by Harry Blackmun working on his draft opinion that summer and into the fall. Despite Douglas's claim that the abortion cases had been thoroughly worked over and considered, Blackmun didn't agree. And despite having been buried in briefs on the subject, he still felt more could be learned and thought about, especially in respect to the medical questions involved in abortion.

During that summer Blackmun returned to the Mayo Clinic in Rochester, Minnesota, where he had spent nine years as the institution's lawyer. There he was invited to use his old office and the clinic's voluminous medical library. For two weeks he did intensive research, concentrating on the medical background he needed to redraft the *Roe* majority opinion addressing Brennan's "core constitutional question." Back in Washington, Blackmun continued working on the abortion cases until the Court's 1973 term began in October.

As the controversial rearguments were held on October 11,

the counsels from Texas and Georgia came away still unsure as to what the outcome would be. But a few days later in the Court's sacrosanct conference room, the justices learned that much had transpired since the original arguments and subsequent conference on the abortion cases. When Blackmun's turn came to speak, he confirmed that his position on the cases remained as it had been in the previous term. He then announced that he was revising both the Georgia and Texas opinions and would soon be circulating the new drafts for his brethren's consideration and comments. Then came a big surprise. When Justice Powell had his turn to speak he simply announced that he was basically with Harry Blackmun on the abortion cases. This meant that, when the tallies of possible votes were complete, the majority of five had become a majority of six to affirm the abortion cases. Justices White and Rehnquist would vote to reverse. But once again the chief justice had not decided how he would vote.

On November 22 Blackmun finally circulated the redrafted opinions he had promised. For several weeks the drafting process continued, with the author revising and rerevising his work, taking into account the comments and suggestions from his colleagues. When complete, the opinions consisted of carefully edited compromises providing each member of the majority with an understanding of what he would be voting for in both the Texas and Georgia cases.

Roe v. Wade, the longer of the two opinions, would become the most important in terms of the effects it would have on abortion laws in practically all the states. The somewhat shorter *Doe v. Bolton* opinion would rule out certain specific restrictions imposed by Georgia's recently adopted abortion reform law, and the decision would affect fewer state laws than would *Roe.*

On December 21, when Justice Blackmun circulated his final drafts for both cases, Justice Douglas promptly announced he was formally joining the revised opinions. Right after Christmas Justices Brennan, Stewart, and Marshall followed suit, and shortly after New Year's Justice Powell joined them. Meanwhile concurring opinions supporting facets of Blackmun's work had been written and circulated by Justices Douglas and Stewart. And in the second week of January Justices White and Rehnquist circulated drafts of dissenting opinions they intended to deliver. The dissenters raised questions about the constitutional basis on which the Blackmun opinions supported the majority decisions, and they deplored what they claimed was an imposition of the Court on the legislative role of the states.

At this point Justice Blackmun hoped the abortion decisions could be publicly announced on January 17, and most of his colleagues agreed; however, one member of the Court, the chief justice, still hadn't revealed where he stood on the decisions. Some of the justices felt his foot-dragging had an ulterior motive connected to President Nixon's second-term inauguration on January 20. The guessing had it that Warren Burger feared the abortion announcement preceding the event would be an untimely, unnecessary affront to the antiabortion president he would be swearing in. True or not, this seemed to be borne out just before the inauguration when Burger suddenly joined the Blackmun opinions. He then claimed he needed a few days to write a brief concurring opinion, and to allow himself time for this he scheduled the announcement date for Monday, January 22, two days after the inauguration. This meant that the High Court's secrecy kept Richard Nixon from knowing that soon after his swearing in, the Court would hand down two abortion cases that he would despise, and the majority would include three of the four justices he had appointed. Furthermore, the decisions would confirm that the president's campaign promises to turn the liberal Warren Court into a conservative Court were not being kept.

14

A Momentous Decision

The Supreme Court's traditional devotion to secrecy hid the abortion cases from the public all the way to the time the decisions would be publicly announced by the justices in the courtroom. That time had been set as 10 A.M. on Monday, January 23, 1973. Until then no one outside of the Court was to know when or how the cases had been decided. The president of the United States was not to know, nor were the people most intimately involved in the cases. In Texas Sarah Weddington, Linda Coffee, and their client, Norma McCorvey (Jane Roe), were not alerted. Nor were Henry Wade, Jay Floyd, or Robert Flowers. In Georgia Margie Hames and her client, Sandra Bensing (Mary Doe), were not informed, nor were Arthur Bolton and Dorothy Beasley. However, only a few hours before the scheduled announcement, the secrecy was violated by *Time* magazine's January 29 issue, which went on the newsstands early in the morning of the twenty-second. A brief article, drawing on undisclosed but informed sources, revealed that the Court was about to overrule nearly every antiabortion law in the country. Chief Justice Burger learned of the scoop—although it remained a scoop for only a couple of hours—and his rising anger was almost more than he could contain as he led the justices into the courtroom at ten o'clock. The large crowd they found waiting to hear the decisions confirmed that word of what was to transpire had spread rapidly.

Four members of the Court were actively involved in the announcement. The chief justice introduced the cases. Justice Blackmun, author of the fifty-one pages that had become "the opinion of the Court" for *Roe v. Wade,* read an eight-page summary of it. And both Justices White and Rehnquist, in an unusual and, in some people's minds, unfriendly act, read their dissenting opinions aloud. But the Blackmun reading was the one that told most clearly what the Court was doing that day. A condensation of what he read follows:

"We forthwith acknowledge our awareness of the sensitive and emotional nature of the abortion controversy, of the vigorous opposing views, even among physicians, and of the deep and seemingly absolute convictions that the subject inspires. One's philosophy, one's experience, one's exposure to the raw edges of human existence, one's religious training, one's attitudes toward life and family and their values, and the moral standards one establishes and seeks to observe, are all likely to influence and to color one's thinking and conclusions about abortion.

"In addition, population growth, pollution, poverty, and racial overtones tend to complicate and not to simplify the problem.

"Our task, of course, is to resolve the issue of constitutional measurement free of emotion and [bias]. We seek earnestly to do this, and, because we do, we have inquired into . . . medical and medical-legal history and what that history reveals about man's attitudes toward the abortion procedures over the centuries. . . .

"The principal thrust of appellant's [Roe's] attack on the Texas statutes is that they improperly invade a right, said to be possessed by the pregnant woman, to choose to terminate her pregnancy. Appellant would discover this right in the concept of personal 'liberty' embodied in the Fourteenth Amendment's due process clause; or in personal, marital, familial, and sexual privacy said to be protected by the Bill of Rights or its penumbras [as established in *Griswold v. Connecticut*] . . .

"The Constitution does not explicitly mention any right of privacy. In a line of decisions, however . . . the Court has recognized that a right of personal privacy, or a guarantee of certain areas or zones of privacy, does exist under the Constitution. . . . The decisions make it clear that . . . the right has some extension to activities relating to marriage . . . procreation . . . contraception . . . family relationships . . . and child rearing and education.

"This right of privacy, whether it be founded in the Fourteenth Amendment's concept of personal liberty and restrictions upon state action, as we feel it is, or . . . in the Ninth Amendment's reservation of rights to the people, is broad enough to encompass a woman's decision whether or not to terminate her pregnancy. The detriment that the State would impose upon the pregnant woman by denying this choice altogether is apparent. Specific and direct harm medically . . . even in early pregnancy may be involved. Maternity, or additional offspring, may force upon the woman a distressful life and future. Psychological harm may be imminent. Mental and physical health may be taxed by child care. There is also the distress, for all concerned, associated with the unwanted child, and there is a problem of bringing a child into a family already unable, psychologically and otherwise, to care for it. In other cases, as in this one, the additional difficulties and continuing stigma of unwed motherhood may be involved. All these are factors the woman and her responsible physician necessarily will consider in consultation.

"On the basis of elements such as these, appellant [Roe] and some *amici* [friends of the court] argue that the woman's right is absolute and that she is entitled to terminate her pregnancy at whatever time, in whatever way, and for whatever reason she alone chooses. With this we do not agree. . . . The Court's decisions recognizing a right of privacy also acknowledge that some state regulation . . . is appropriate. [A] State may properly assert important interests in safeguarding health, in maintaining medical standards, and in protecting potential life. At some point in pregnancy, these respective interests become sufficiently compelling [to regulate] the factors that govern the abortion decision. . . .

"We, therefore, conclude that the right of personal privacy includes the abortion decision, but that this right is not unqualified and must be considered against important state interests in regulation. . . .

"Appellant [Roe] . . . claims an absolute right that bars any state imposition of criminal penalties in the area [of abortion]. Appellee [Wade] argues that the State's determination to recognize and protect [life before birth] from and after conception constitutes a compelling state interest. . . . We do not agree fully with either formulation.

"The appellee and certain *amici* argue that the fetus is a

'person' within the language and meaning of the Fourteenth Amendment. In support of this, they outline at length and in detail the well-known facts of fetal development. If this suggestion of personhood is established, the appellant's case, of course, collapses, for the fetus' right to life is then guaranteed specifically by the Amendment. . . . [But] in short, the unborn have never been recognized in the law as persons in the whole sense.

"In view of all this, we do not agree that, by adopting one theory of life, Texas may override the rights of the pregnant woman that are at stake. We repeat, however, that the State does have an important and legitimate interest in preserving and protecting the health of the pregnant woman. . . . Each [of these state interests] grows substantially as the woman approaches term and, at a point during pregnancy each becomes 'compelling.'

"With respect to the State's important and legitimate interest in the health of the mother, the 'compelling' point, in the light of present medical knowledge, is approximately the end of the first trimester. . . .

"This means, on the other hand, that, for the period prior to this 'compelling' point, the attending physician, in consultation with his patient, is free to determine, without regulation by the State, that in his medical judgment, the patient's pregnancy should be terminated. If that decision is reached, the judgment may be effectuated by an abortion free of interference by the State. . . .

"With respect to the State's important and legitimate interest in potential life, the compelling point is viability. This is so because the fetus presumably has the capability of meaningful life outside the mother's womb. State regulation protective of fetal life after viability thus has both logical and biological justification. If the State is interested in protecting fetal life after viability, it may go so far as to [outlaw] abortion during that period, except when it is necessary to preserve the life or health of the mother. . . .

"To summarize and repeat:

"1. A state criminal abortion statute of the current Texas type, that excepts from criminality only a *life-saving* procedure on behalf of the mother, without regard to pregnancy stage and without recognition of the other interests involved, is violative of the due process clause of the Fourteenth Amendment.

"(a) For the stage prior to approximately the end of the first trimester, the abortion decision and its effectuation must be left to the medical judgment of the pregnant woman's attending physician.

"(b) For the stage subsequent to approximately the end of the first trimester, the State, in promoting its interest in the health of the mother, may, if it chooses, regulate the abortion procedure in ways that are reasonably related to maternal health.

"(c) For the stage subsequent to viability, the State, in promoting its interest in the potentiality of human life, may, if it chooses, regulate, and even [outlaw], abortion except where it is necessary, in appropriate medical judgment, for the preservation of the life or health of the woman.

"Measured against these standards, Article 1196 of the Texas Penal Code, in restricting abortions to those . . . for saving the life of the mother, sweeps too broadly. The statute makes no distinction between abortions performed early in pregnancy and those performed later, and it limits to a single reason, 'saving' the mother's life, the legal justification for the procedure. The statute, therefore, cannot survive the constitutional attack made upon it. . . ."

The Texas law did not survive the attack made upon it by Sarah Weddington and Linda Coffee, nor did state abortion laws all across the nation. With the conditions set forth by Harry Blackmun, abortion in America became a matter of personal privacy and personal choice protected by the Constitution of the United States. That day in 1973 *Roe v. Wade* came down as a momentous decision which swept across America, divided the nation, and traumatically changed the last quarter of the twentieth century.

15

The Deep Divide

On Monday morning, January 22, 1973, Sarah Weddington went to her new office at the state capitol in Austin, Texas. In the fall elections she had won a seat in the Texas House of Representatives, and that morning she was preparing for the week's legislative sessions. Suddenly two important telephone calls came into her office. She took the first, which came from the law office she shared with her husband, Ron. Their secretary said a reporter from the *New York Times* had called seeking a comment from Sarah about *Roe v. Wade.*

"Is there some particular reason she could have a comment about it today?" the secretary had asked.

"Yes," the reporter replied. "The decision was announced in Washington this morning at ten."

"How?" the secretary asked, warily.

"She won."

When Sarah Weddington caught her breath after hearing the stunning message, she took the second call. This one, from the NBC *Today* show, confirmed her victory—and so began the deluge of calls seeking comments and offering congratulations. Of course, one came from Linda Coffee who had heard the news on her car radio. Both lawyers were overjoyed by what had happened. "We could not get over the fact," Weddington wrote years later, "that we, two young women lawyers not long out of law school, relatively inexperienced, who few people thought had a chance, had contributed to winning a crucial Supreme Court decision."

While their victory kept Sarah Weddington busy with telephone calls and visitors at her capitol office, the most historic message of the occasion arrived at the office shared with her husband. It came from Washington, a telegram from Michael Rodak, Jr., Clerk, Supreme Court of the United States, reading as follows: "TO SARAH WEDDINGTON, WEDDINGTON AND WEDDINGTON, 709 FOURTEENTH STREET, AUSTIN, TEXAS. JUDGMENT ROE AGAINST WADE TODAY AFFIRMED IN PART AND REVERSED IN PART. JUDGMENT DOE AGAINST BOLTON MODIFIED AND AFFIRMED. OPINIONS AIRMAILED."

But what about Jane Roe? the reporters wanted to know. Who and where was she? But they couldn't find out. Her lawyers would not violate her anonymity, so the media had no way of contacting the now famous plaintiff. For that matter, her lawyers themselves had no luck in contacting her. They had a telephone number provided many months earlier by Norma McCorvey's father, but now no one answered.

Actually Norma McCorvey was away, working from dawn to dusk at a thriving business cleaning and painting apartments around Dallas. She had established the business with her roommate, Connie Gonzales, and they had called it N. L. McCorvey & Company. Returning home late that evening, McCorvey picked up the newspaper delivered earlier and was startled to see that Lyndon Johnson had died, but then she was much more startled to see a small front-page article reporting that the Supreme Court of the United States had legalized abortion. The seven-to-two vote favored an anonymous petitioner in a case from Texas titled *Roe v. Wade.* McCorvey, who had not revealed her involvement in the case to Gonzales, pointed out the article and noted that the petitioner was Jane Roe. Gonzales hardly paid any attention until McCorvey asked, "How would you like to meet Jane Roe?" What a facetious question, Gonzales thought, as she replied, "We don't know anybody like that." No more was said about it that evening.

But for Norma McCorvey the news quickly ceased being a joking matter. She realized that the case she had agreed to, but had generally ignored, now made her the winner in a major decision of the Supreme Court legalizing abortion all across America. She had difficulty sleeping that night and said nothing about it at work the next day. But that evening McCorvey could no longer keep the secret from Gonzales and told her the whole story in confidence. McCorvey confessed she had become terrified for fear that a lie she had told her lawyers might now get them all into very serious trouble. She had told them her pregnancy had resulted from being raped, which wasn't true. To McCorvey that fear was very real, but unnecessary. She had never understood that *Roe v. Wade* was a class action, so that Roe did not stand for Norma McCorvey alone, but for all women denied the legal right to abortions.

While their petitioner kept to herself, Sarah Weddington, Linda Coffee, and friends celebrated Jane Roe's extraordinary victory. But their elation didn't last, for they quickly grew fearful that the Court's decision might be short-lived, and the newly legalized act of abortion might soon return to being a crime. The lawyers knew that a lot of people would be opposed to what had happened, but the vehemence coming from the hard core of the opposition could hardly have been anticipated.

When opinion polls began testing the public reaction to *Roe v. Wade,* they revealed that the country was sharply divided, and it remained so. On the decision's first anniversary, for example, a Gallup poll found the American public almost evenly divided, with 47 percent favoring *Roe* and 44 percent opposed. But the opponents hadn't waited for the anniversary to fight the decision. When it was announced, *Roe* acted like cold water in the face for those people already fighting abortion on the state level. *Roe* galvanized them, and they hit the track running for a major battle on the national level.

In the struggle that ensued, the cause of the antiabortion forces became known as "prolife." At first these organizations were often supported by, or even run by, the Catholic Church, but later the antiabortion forces became strongly associated with fundamentalist Christians and conservative politicians referred to as the "New Right"—cohorts who often made Catholic leaders very uncomfortable. Those in favor of *Roe,* mostly feminist organizations and people supporting birth control and abortion rights, did not like the proabortion label, so they promoted the term "prochoice." This increased their numbers by including people who were not necessarily for abortion but granted that pregnant women now had the right to choose whether or not they would have an abortion.

As the prolife leaders planned their attack on *Roe v. Wade,* they had only two ways to eliminate the decision by legal means and return to the antiabortion laws on the books in most of the states. They could try to work out an amendment to the Constitution of the United States that would override *Roe* and forbid abortion. Or they could do everything politically possible to (1) change the makeup of the federal courts by working to elect U.S. presidents committed to filling vacancies with lower-court judges and Supreme Court justices who would vote to overrule *Roe v. Wade*, and (2) test the limits of *Roe* by promoting state laws restricting access to abortions to the extent that the High Court would permit.

Early on, a constitutional amendment seemed the swiftest way to deal a death blow to what the Court had done. This effort got under way within six months when seven U.S. senators, led by James Buckley of New York, introduced an abortion-banning constitutional amendment in the Senate and began what at best would be a long, difficult process. Two thirds of the members in both the Senate and House of Representatives would have to vote favorably on the amendment. If they did, the amendment would then have to be ratified by three quarters of the nation's state legislatures. This meant hundreds of federal and state lawmakers would have to favor changing the Constitution, something that history showed was not very likely to happen. Nevertheless the *Roe* opponents felt they could succeed because public opposition to the Court's decision would motivate the lawmakers to carry it out. But they were wrong. The Buckley amendment, and later versions of it, failed time and again to win Congressional approval, to say nothing of winning in the states. However, politicians were forever plagued by prolifers asking if they were for or against the amendment. It became a quick test to see if a politician was or wasn't with them.

Meanwhile the prochoice leaders were not resting on their laurels. They immediately began to consolidate their victory in a practical way. Planned Parenthood and the National Association for the Repeal of Abortion Laws concentrated on opening clinics to augment existing health facilities in providing safe, affordable abortions. The two organizations also conducted seminars around the country to help develop programs and staffs to implement the new freedom provided by *Roe v. Wade.* The need for all this became evident right away, as the demand for abortions increased far more than had been expected. A subsequent survey revealed that in 1973, the year of the decision, three quarters of a million legal abortions were performed in the United States. And on January 6, 1974, a *New York Times* survey found abortions were now in the "mainstream of modern medical care" throughout the United States. This trend continued, and in 1980 a survey found that over one and a half million legal abortions were performed in the country, thereby terminating one of every four pregnancies. Subsequent studies came up with comparable results throughout the 1980s.

The rising tide of abortions was countered, but not diminished, by a growing number of opponents in more than a half dozen prolife organizations nationally. These included Americans United for Life, the National Right to Life Committee, Operation Rescue, American Life Lobby, National Pro-Life Political Action Committee, Rescue America–National, Army of God, and Lambs of Christ. Many members of these organizations were intensely devout activists whose main goal was to have *Roe v. Wade* eliminated while rendering it ineffective in the meantime.

The prolife political presence was most evident each year on January 22, the anniversary of *Roe*'s announcement by the Supreme Court. On the first anniversary, six thousand protesters arrived in Washington to petition Congress to approve the Buckley constitutional amendment. The number of protesters increased by the tens of thousands as the *Roe* anniversaries went by. Sixty-five thousand rallied in Washington on the third anniversary. The number varied from year to year but peaked on the seventeenth anniversary, with an estimated two hundred thousand arriving in the nation's capital.

The greatest prolife political victory came in 1980 with the election of President Ronald Reagan, who unequivocally supported a constitutional amendment banning abortion and the appointment of prolife justices to the Supreme Court. In the nine years since President Nixon's last appointments only one new justice had been appointed, John Paul Stevens. Nominated by President Ford, Stevens replaced the retiring William O. Douglas and, as it turned out, he respected *Roe v. Wade,* thereby preserving the seven-to-two majority favoring the decision.

But then Ronald Reagan had the opportunity to make three appointments to the Court. All three replaced retiring justices who had originally voted for the decision, Warren E. Burger, Potter Stewart, and William F. Powell. Their places were taken by Sandra Day O'Connor, Antonin Scalia, and Anthony M. Kennedy. Reagan was also responsible for elevating William Rehnquist to chief justice. Justice Scalia became a firm opponent of *Roe,* while O'Connor and Kennedy turned out to favor its preservation. A staunch enemy of the abortion decision, Robert H. Bork, was nominated by President Reagan, but after his bitter confirmation hearings the nominee failed to be confirmed by the Senate.

While some prolifers concentrated on changing the Supreme Court in their favor, others promoted state laws limiting access to abortions then being performed by the thousands. In a number of instances they succeeded, with, for example, laws that would keep a wife from having an abortion without her husband's consent, or allow a single woman under age eighteen to have an abortion only if her parents consented. Such laws were challenged in federal courts by prochoice organizations, especially by Planned Parenthood. They were usually struck down in the lower courts or by the Supreme Court. Then the High Court heard a case from Akron, Ohio, and in 1983 the decision ruled against an array of state and local curbs on abortion. If the decision had agreed to the curbs, it might have simultaneously dealt a fatal blow to *Roe v. Wade.*

The decision led President Reagan to express his profound disappointment over the Court's stand, and he called on Congress to act on what the justices were doing to the state laws. However, only a couple of days later he suffered another disappointment when the Senate defeated a constitutional amendment asserting that the right to an abortion is not secured by the Constitution.

Reagan's disappointments continued throughout his presidency, which had begun with hope for an end to *Roe v. Wade.* When it became clear this wouldn't happen, many prolife activists, turning away from politics, increased their efforts to deter women from having abortions and doctors from performing them. Then harassments at clinics increased both in number and severity, including bombings which spread across the country. An opening assault occurred in February 1984, when several pipe bombs exploded outside a clinic in Norfolk, Virginia, breaking windows but causing no personal injuries. The yearlong series of bombings that followed was characterized by the *New York Times* as a form of domestic terrorism. The bombers' crescendo for 1984 came on Christmas Day, with a series of explosions that ripped through three offices where abortions were performed in Pensacola, Florida. A few days later President Reagan finally condemned the extensive bombings, but he failed to propose how the government might help stop them.

And guns came with the bombs. One of the early, well-publicized shots was fired on the night of February 28, 1984. The author of *Roe v. Wade,* Justice Harry Blackmun, and his wife were at home in their apartment in Arlington, Virginia, when a bullet smashed through the window of the living room where they were reading. Four months earlier Blackmun had received a threatening letter from someone in the antiabortion organization Army of God. The FBI was still trying to find the author when they had to investigate the shooting. They discovered the bullet lodged in a sofa but never found the gunman or the letter writer.

The most visible of all the antiabortion organizations, Operation Rescue, formed in the late eighties by Randall Terry, was headquartered in Binghamton, New York. Its modus operandi, more military than political, was to blockade abortion clinics to keep women from using them. Operation Rescue gained national notoriety as Terry's growing army of followers blockaded clinics in numerous other cities. In 1989 their tactics led to more dramatic blockades in Woodbridge, New Jersey, where eight protesters, fastened together with chains around their necks and legs, entered an abortion clinic and kept it from operating for twelve hours before their arrest.

The prevalence of these disruptive, violent protests was shown by a study revealing that from 1977 to 1989 antiabortion extremists had bombed or set fire to 117 clinics in the United States. Another 224 had been threatened, while almost that many had been invaded or vandalized. The worst was yet to come, but briefly in 1989 prolife leaders had reason to think their battle might have been won at the Supreme Court of the United States.

In the spring of 1989 the Court scheduled oral arguments on *Webster v. Reproductive Health Services,* a case that had come on appeal from Missouri where a state law with very stringent curbs on abortion had been declared unconstitutional by a lower federal court. The law had serious conflicts with *Roe v. Wade.* Its preamble, for example, declared that the life of each human being begins at conception, and as much as possible, the state of Missouri would treat the fetus as a person with the rights enjoyed by all persons. The main part of the law said that (1) no abortion could be performed in a public hospital or facility; (2) no publicly employed personnel could perform an abortion, doctors included; and (3) after twenty weeks of a pregnancy a woman could not obtain an abortion without a test to determine if the fetus could survive outside the womb. The appeal came to the Supreme Court with its new Reagan appointees. It was feared they might take the opportunity to overrule *Roe v. Wade* as they accepted the abortion curbs in the Missouri law.

Prochoice leaders recognized the serious implications of the case for the survival of *Roe,* and they went on the offensive. On April 9, 1989, prior to oral arguments on *Webster,* up to six hundred thousand women marched and rallied outside the Supreme Court in behalf of *Roe v. Wade.* The defenders of *Roe* also contributed heavily to the amicus briefs, which added up to a record number submitted to the Court. On July 3, when the *Webster* decision was announced, another tumultuous crowd, both for and against *Roe,* waited on the Court steps for the results.

The initial news reports were confusing because the decision consisted of a mixed bag of several opinions. Sarah Weddington, waiting in an ABC studio in Texas, was ready to comment, but nothing she heard made the results clear. One report frightened her, for it revealed that Chief Justice Rehnquist, who had provided one of the two original votes against *Roe,* had written the opinion of the Court. She feared *Roe* had been overruled—but it hadn't. That was confirmed by four words in Rehnquist's opinion stating: "We leave it undisturbed." While *Webster* left *Roe* standing—although tottering—it also left the Missouri law in place with its abortion restrictions essentially intact, and this could now invite other states to pass similar laws. Justice Blackmun's dissenting opinion let it be known he was extremely upset by the decision. "For today at least," he said, "the law of abortion stands undisturbed. For today the women of this Nation still retain the liberty to control their destinies. But the signs are evident and very ominous, and a chill wind blows."

Prolifers had a mixed reaction to *Webster.* While one leader announced, "*Roe* is dead!" others felt *Webster* had done nothing for their cause. Prochoice leaders agreed with Justice

Blackmun. *Roe* was still alive, despite *Webster*'s having delivered a near-fatal blow, and the future looked bad.

However, *Webster* set off an alarm that prochoice forces needed, a warning that supporters of *Roe v. Wade* had to go on the offensive. They did and were as effective as their prolife counterparts—or more so. Proof of this was soon evident in the Republican party's misfortune of 1989.

Both Presidents Reagan and Bush had committed the party to the prolife side of the sharp divide over abortion. That commitment became very costly in the 1989 midterm elections, when a number of influential Republican women abandoned their party's rigid prolife stand. On election day the party took a drubbing at the polls. It was so serious that party leaders urged Republicans to become more tolerant of abortion rights. Nevertheless, when President Bush tried for a second term, he ran on a prolife platform that once more supported the elusive constitutional amendment banning abortion. The party's most famous conservative, Barry Goldwater, sounding like a classic liberal, charged that the president's antiabortion stand could sink the Republican Party. Exit polls (voters interviewed right after they had voted) indicated that Goldwater had a point. George Bush's antiabortion stand in 1992 contributed to his defeat and the election of a prochoice president, Bill Clinton.

During his presidency, President Bush filled two vacancies on the Supreme Court, having been assured that both nominees were conservatives who would vote to overrule *Roe.* They were David H. Souter and Clarence Thomas, and they replaced two firm defenders of *Roe,* William J. Brennan and Thurgood Marshall.

Regardless of George Bush's efforts to rid the country of

Roe, prolife activists, unwilling to wait for it to happen, continued their harassment of abortion doctors and patients. In fact they intensified their protests nationwide, with a horrendous six weeks in Wichita, Kansas, during the summer of 1991. Operation Rescue summoned its followers, and they came in droves to Wichita from all across the nation. They virtually tore the city apart with mass blockades of abortion clinics. As usual, they defied court orders and were arrested for contempt of court in great numbers, which overwhelmed the local jails.

The national publicity of these events stimulated the increasing numbers of prochoice activists, and in many states they were able to slow down passage of new antiabortion legislation prompted by *Webster*'s approval of Missouri's law. However, some tough new statutes were adopted, one of which was destined to play a role in a landmark case in the struggle over *Roe* itself. It was passed and signed into law in 1989 by Governor Robert P. Casey of Pennsylvania, and included antiabortion restrictions typical of those appearing elsewhere. The law was soon contested by a Pennsylvania chapter of Planned Parenthood, and in 1992 the case was heard by the Supreme Court of the United States on appeal from a lower federal court.

Planned Parenthood of Southeastern Pennsylvania v. Casey became the case following *Webster* that could serve for the Court to overrule *Roe v. Wade.* When *Webster* was decided, Chief Justice Rehnquist and three justices, White, Scalia, and Kennedy, indicated their readiness to overrule *Roe.* They needed only one more vote to make a majority, and now the chief justice was sure it would come from the newest justice, Clarence Thomas, a conservative and a Roman Catholic.

Prochoice leaders, realizing that *Casey* put *Roe* in mortal danger, mounted the largest demonstration on the abortion issue ever seen in Washington. The police estimated a half million people showed up, but the organizers put it at seven hundred thousand. Of considerable political significance was the fact that the huge crowd included the three leading contenders for the presidential candidacy of the Democratic party: Edmund Brown, Paul Tsongas, and Bill Clinton.

After the oral arguments were heard on the Pennsylvania case, the chief justice remained sure he had a majority of five to overrule *Roe,* or even of six if Justice Souter joined the group. However, Souter's position on the abortion decision was still unknown. From the time of his nomination through his confirmation hearings he had declined to say how he would vote on *Roe,* indicating he hadn't resolved the question and wouldn't until faced with it on the Court. This explanation earned Souter the nickname of the "Stealth Nominee." Nevertheless, the chief justice, certain of five votes, took it upon himself to draft the majority opinion.

But that opinion fell apart before completion of the draft, when Justice Kennedy abruptly joined Justices Souter and Sandra Day O'Connor in a trio that had an agenda different from Rehnquist's. Meeting privately in Souter's office, the trio drafted a statement in which Justices Blackmun and Stevens concurred. That statement, now supported by a five-vote plurality, became the opinion of the Court. It was a masterfully constructed judicial document, which at last reflected the making up of David Souter's mind. When *Casey* was announced on Monday, June 29, 1992, the opinion was presented in a most unusual way. Ordinarily, a lengthy opinion like *Casey*'s would have been summarized or excerpted, and read aloud by the author. But this time it was presented by the trio, each reading a large section aloud—O'Connor first, Kennedy second, and Souter last.

The opinion began: "Liberty finds no refuge in a jurisprudence [science of law] of doubt. Yet nineteen years after our holding that the Constitution protects a woman's right to terminate her pregnancy in its early stages, *Roe v. Wade,* that definition is still questioned. Joining the respondents as *amicus curiae,* the United States [specifically the Reagan and Bush administrations], as it has done in five other cases in the last decade, again asks us to overrule *Roe.*"

The opinion made it clear that *Roe v. Wade* was not being overruled. To the contrary, *Casey* was reaffirming *Roe*'s "essential holding": that a woman's right to terminate her pregnancy in its early stages is protected by the Constitution. The following is a synopsis of how the opinion supported that position:

The authors, while expressing concern for the fate of the 1973 abortion decision, also expressed alarm over what the Court was doing to itself in regard to the decision. They pointed out that *Roe,* as originally decided, had been solidly based in the Constitution. Moreover, since 1973 *Roe* had worked well, with millions of women accepting the new freedom, not only as it pertained to abortion, but even to their improved social and economic status. Nevertheless, the High Court, despite this success, had not indicated it remained firmly behind the decision. Instead it conveyed an image of doubt in respect to *Roe v. Wade.* This, in turn, undermined a doctrine essential for a strong, credible judiciary, the doctrine of *stare decisis* (a Latin term meaning "to abide by, or adhere to, decided cases"). The failing in the greatest court in the land was cause for alarm because it contributed to the divisiveness that had plagued the nation for many years over *Roe v. Wade.* It thereby invited continual political pressure on the judicial branch of the government, which was meant to make decisions based on the Constitution, not on the political winds of the day.

The *Casey* opinion concluded, "A decision to overrule *Roe*'s essential holding under the existing circumstances would . . . [be] at the cost of both profound and unnecessary damage to the Court's legitimacy, and to the Nation's commitment to the rule of law. It is therefore imperative to adhere to the essence of *Roe*'s original decision, and we do so today."

If Justice Souter's leadership in the *Casey* decision surprised and disappointed the prolife president who nominated him and the senators who confirmed him, it was because they had not looked carefully enough into his record as a New Hampshire judge. He was a conservative, but one who believed in standing by and preserving past decisions that were soundly made. He had been a strong advocate of *stare decisis.* That might have foretold that the Stealth Nominee would be unlikely to favor overruling *Roe v. Wade.*

Although *Casey* would eventually be recognized as a landmark decision for rescuing *Roe v. Wade* from the brink of defeat, this was not immediately clear. Both sides of the endless abortion debate felt half satisfied and half disappointed. Prochoice leaders were glad that *Roe* had survived but unhappy that *Casey* did not completely rule out the Pennsylvania law's abortion restrictions. Their opponents had the opposite opinion: They were glad that the restrictions remained but unhappy that *Roe v. Wade* still survived.

In historical terms, however, the firm reaffirmation of *Roe* was what made *Casey* a landmark decision. And *Roe*'s continued survival was soon strengthened when Justice Byron R. White retired in March 1993. After casting one of the two votes against *Roe* in 1973, White remained over the next twenty-one years a potential vote for overruling the decision. He was replaced by Justice Ruth Bader Ginsburg, President Clinton's first appointment to the Court, and the second woman ever to become a justice. In her confirmation hearings, Ginsburg had voiced strong support for the constitutional right to abortion.

But while *Casey* and the change of justices enhanced *Roe v. Wade*'s longevity, it did not heal the division splitting America apart over abortion. Indeed, *Roe*'s survival may have contributed to a frightening escalation of antiabortion rhetoric and violence. This was dramatically pointed up on March 10, 1993, in Pensacola, Florida.

That day Dr. David Gunn, who had been dividing his time among six abortion clinics in Florida, Georgia, and Alabama, was shot and killed by a prolife activist, Michael Griffin. Then, shortly after the murder, another prolife activist, Paul Hill, flew from Pensacola to New York and appeared on NBC's *Donahue* show. There Hill, a former minister in conservative denominations of the Presbyterian Church, defended Griffin's actions. He maintained that Dr. Gunn deserved to die, because he was a murderer of "children," an abortionist, who had to be stopped. In the next year or so Hill appeared on other talk shows, including ABC's *Nightline,* and continued to defend homicide as a legitimate way of stopping the murders of children by abortion doctors. He claimed that the Bible, according to his reading of it, justified the killings that he advocated. After sixteen months of his public statements, Paul Hill practiced what he preached. He murdered Dr. Gunn's replacement, Dr. John Bayard Britton, and his volunteer "safety escort," James H. Barrett, as they arrived at a Pensacola abortion clinic. While Griffin had been convicted and sentenced to life in prison, the jury that found Hill guilty of the two murders recommended that he be executed in Florida's electric chair.

These three murders, and the attempted murder of a Wichita doctor by a prolife protester from Oregon, exposed the entire prolife movement to public outrage over what was happening. Their leaders denied having anything to do with the killings, only to be accused of having prompted the crimes by their rhetoric—forever referring to abortion as murder of children, describing doctors performing abortions as "baby killers," and claiming the country was witnessing an "abortion Holocaust." The charges against such rhetoric became more credible on the next to last day of 1994.

This time a deeply disturbed young loner, John C. Salvi III, entered two abortion clinics in Brookline, Massachusetts, and shot and killed two young women employees and wounded five other people. These killings during the holiday season deeply affected religious leaders across the country. One of the strongest opponents of abortion among the nation's Catholic bishops, Bernard Cardinal Law, the archbishop of Boston, declared a moratorium on sidewalk vigils at abortion clinics. He asked that prochoice supporters not blame "the unconscionable acts of a few [on the] millions who advocate a prolife position." In nearby Manchester, New Hampshire, Bishop Leo O'Neil said, "While I fully understand that peaceful protest serves a valid purpose, I believe this time we must step back for a while." He asked that prolife supporters work using "the calm voice of reason, quietly, intelligently, steadfastly, logically presenting the truth that all life is a gift that must be respected."

The slaying of Dr. Gunn had an immediate effect on the Congress of the United States, and it soon passed a bill that would make bombing, arson, blockades of abortion clinics, and shootings and threats of violence against doctors and nurses performing abortions a federal crime. In May 1994 President Clinton signed the bill, which became the Freedom of Access to Clinic Entrances Act. Furthermore, the Supreme Court unanimously ruled earlier that year that federal racketeering laws could be used by abortion clinics and others to sue violent prolife organizations for damages and force them to pay up to three times the value of the damages. With these legal tools, prochoice organizations, doctors, and clinics began winning cases against antiabortion protestors who were disrupting their abortion services, and the juries involved ordered the defendants to pay huge sums in damages. In Houston, Texas, for example, a state jury ordered two prolife organizations, Operation Rescue and Rescue America, to pay a Planned Parenthood clinic over a million dollars in punitive damages. The leaders of the two organizations were each ordered to pay, out of their own pockets, one hundred and fifty thousand dollars of the award. Then Dr. Norman Tompkins, a Dallas obstetrician-gynecologist, won a suit against seven individuals and three groups who, he charged, had driven him out of business by following and harassing him while threatening to kill him and his wife. A jury awarded him over eight and one half million dollars to be paid by the individuals and organizations. These penalties were serious blows that began to deter antiabortion protests relying on tactics that now violated federal laws.

Given all that had happened over the years because of Jane Roe's victory against Henry Wade in 1973—the deep divisiveness it caused, the political turmoil, the vehemence, the disruptions, the violence even to the point of murders—it often surprised American citizens to learn how many abortions continued to be performed and for whom in the United States. The statistics were regularly compiled by the Alan Guttmacher Institute in New York. Here are excerpts from the institute's findings:

- The United States has one of the highest abortion rates among developed countries.
- From 1973 through 1992 more than twenty-eight million legal abortions took place in the United States.
- More than 50 percent of the pregnancies among American women are unintended—one half of these are terminated by abortion.
- Eighteen- to nineteen-year-old women have the highest abortion rate.
- Unmarried women are five times more likely to have an abortion.
- Poor women are about three times more likely to have abortions than women who are financially better off.
- Catholic women are about as likely to obtain an abortion as are all women nationally, while Protestants and Jews are less likely. Catholic women are 30 percent more likely than Protestants to have abortions.

- One in six abortion patients in 1987 described herself as a born-again or Evangelical Christian; they are half as likely as other women to have an abortion.

The institute's findings, from the *Roe v. Wade* decision in 1973 almost to the end of the century, told of how tightly *Roe*'s "essential holding" had been woven into the nation's social fabric and of how difficult this may have become for the vast numbers of people who still sincerely believed the decision was wrong.

Epilogue
Changes and Exchanges

On August 12, 1995, a *New York Times* headline read: NEW TWIST FOR A LANDMARK CASE: ROE V. WADE BECOMES ROE V. ROE. Nothing had happened to the 1973 abortion decision; however, the *Roe* petitioner, Norma McCorvey, had abruptly switched to prolife from prochoice. In March 1995 McCorvey was working for a Dallas abortion clinic when the national headquarters of Operation Rescue moved into an adjoining office, a location its president described as being "at the killing center, at the gates of hell." McCorvey was "horrified," but not for long, for she soon made friends with the neighboring president, the Reverend Flip Benham. Then she became a born-again Christian, with Benham baptizing her in a backyard swimming pool. Also she quit her clinic job to go to work for Operation Rescue, explaining, "I'm prolife. I think I have always been prolife. I just didn't know it."

But over the twenty-two years since *Roe v. Wade* was decided, McCorvey had remained prochoice. This was clear in 1994 when her book came out, titled *I Am Roe: My Life, Roe v. Wade, and Freedom of Choice.* She dedicated it "For all the Jane Does [*sic*] who died for Choice," and ended the text with a reprint of a speech she had frequently delivered. Her peroration read, "People of all nations who are pro-choice and profamily, stand up and be counted. Support pro-choice candidates who are running for office. Write your state legislators and congressmen and congresswomen. Let them know exactly how you feel. Rally and demonstrate in every country and state. Let the United States Supreme Court and our government hear our voices: SILENCE NO MORE! WE WILL NOT GO BACK!"

Then why did she abandon choice for life? It would have no legal impact because *Roe* was a class action, with Jane Roe symbolizing all women facing a comparable plight. Some people felt McCorvey switched to get more public attention than choice leaders were providing. Or maybe she acted out of fear for her personal safety. Or she might truly have been motivated by her new religion. However, there were indications that she really had not become a bona fide, 100 percent prolifer.

The *New York Times* article on McCorvey's changeover noted: "Just when and why and indeed even how fundamentally her mind changed on the abortion issue remains open to question. As abortion-rights advocates quickly pointed out . . . Ms. McCorvey could still be called 'pro-choice': she said this week that she still believed that 'a woman has a right to have an abortion, a safe and legal abortion, in the first trimester' of pregnancy."

Moreover, McCorvey stated that in joining Operation Rescue she would not participate in the organization's confrontations with women entering clinics. When reporters called her home for interviews, they heard only a recorded message: "Hi and thanks for all your calls. I really do appreciate them. There will be no press statements; there will be no more public appearances from me. I am going to be regular person Norma McCorvey. Thank you very much."

If by chance McCorvey held to her dual, prolife-prochoice position—doubtful as it might be—she would have settled on an unpublicized middle ground with a great many other Americans. While they didn't think about labels, they were essentially both prolife and prochoice. On the one hand, the thought of abortion made them uncomfortable, and they didn't like to talk about it, except to say they were against it, thus prolife. On the other hand, many of them respected the constitutional right to abortion that *Roe* had gained for women who chose to use it. Furthermore these citizens were often shocked by the prolifers' harassments, arsons, bombings, blockades, and murders directed at abortion clinics and their doctors and patients. And certainly they wished both sides would settle their angry, divisive quarreling with "the calm voice of reason" called for by the bishop of Manchester after the Brookline clinic murders.

Actually, when Norma McCorvey made her move, a relatively new abortion organization was trying to heal the bitter differences over abortion, and its first public-policy statement was issued one week after McCorvey made her announcement. The organization, the Common Ground Network for Life and Choice, was started in St. Louis in 1992, and by 1995 it had spread to at least twenty cities, from Boston to Denver, to Minneapolis and to the hotbed of violent protests, Pensacola, Florida.

The Common Ground Network grew out of the 1989 Supreme Court case from Missouri, *Webster v. Reproductive Health Services,* which came close to overruling *Roe v. Wade.* The two prime movers of the new organization, Andrew F. Puzder and B. J. Isaacson-Jones, had been on opposing sides of *Webster.* Puzder had helped draft the Missouri abortion restrictions at the heart of the case, and Ms. Isaacson-Jones had been the executive director of the St. Louis family planning clinic, Reproductive Health Services, that sued the state, trying to overturn the restrictions. Subsequently *Webster*'s two opponents got together to see what might be done to bridge the bitter divisions that kept the opposing abortion forces from ever talking over their differences.

They found at least one common ground where both sides might come together. The idea was to work toward reducing, if not completely eliminating, the great numbers of abortions in America each year. Prochoice leaders had frequently expressed their dislike for abortion, and prolifers might compromise on reducing abortions, hoping it might lead to no abortions. The Common Ground Steering Committee's first policy paper issued in Washington discussed adoption as an alternative to abortion and suggested what the government might do to make it acceptable and more available. As expected, promoting adoptions to cut down on abortions had opponents on both sides of the divide, but for once there was an organization for both life and choice ready to talk over the issue calmly and reasonably. And numerous other grounds could be found where the two sides might come together without harassment, threats, suits, and all the other adversary acts that led to bitterness on a road to nowhere.

In the month of Norma McCorvey's switch, another sign of

the changing tone of abortion rhetoric showed up in *The Atlantic Monthly* magazine. The cover, with a painting of our sixteenth president, featured an article titled: "How Lincoln Might Have Dealt with Abortion, A Pro-choice, Anti-abortion Approach." The author, George McKenna, a political science teacher at the City College of New York, was a prolife supporter. His article compared America's most divisive issue of all time, that of slavery, with the invective over abortion. McKenna reviewed how Lincoln dealt with the problem from the mid-1850s on into the Civil War when he was attempting to save the Union and did not let his deep moral opposition to slavery tear the country apart. He did so by tolerating slavery while trying to restrict and discourage it, all with concern for public sentiment and the good of the nation. McKenna felt that antiabortion leaders might draw a lesson from Lincoln's effort.

"The lesson for prolife advocates," he wrote, "is that they need to take the time to lay out their case. They may hope for an immediate end to abortion . . . but their emphasis, I believe, should be on making clear to others why they have reached the conclusions that they have reached. They need to reason with skeptics and listen more carefully to critics. They need to demand less and explain more. Whatever the outcome, that would surely contribute to the process of reasonable public discourse."

The last two sentences of McKenna's article said: "Abortion, a tragedy in everyone's estimation, will continue to darken our prospect until we find practical ways of dealing with it in order to make it rare. But before we can hope to do that, we have to start talking with one another honestly, in honest language."

This article from a prolife supporter offered a refreshing change from the bombastic antiabortion rhetoric heard for many years. If, in fact, the volume was being turned down, the reason may have been found in an article by David J. Garrow one week after the murders of two abortion clinic workers in Brookline, Massachusetts, Shannon Lowney and Leanne Nichols. Garrow was the author of two major books, one on the civil rights movement and the other on the development of *Roe v. Wade.*

Titled "A Deadly, Dying Fringe," his article in the *New York Times* drew an analogy between what happened in the civil rights era of the 1960s and the tragic murders between 1993 and 1995 of the abortion rights era. In the sixties, Garrow pointed out, several murders were committed in the South by Ku Klux Klan–sponsored extremists when it became clear that segregationists were losing their political and legal battles. With the passage of the Civil Rights Act of 1964 and the Voting Rights Act of 1965, and the large-scale registration of black voters, the cause of segregation was under attack. Many people feared the killings in the South showed that the Klan's reign of terror was gaining, but the opposite proved to be the case, and in time it was realized the slayings signaled the segregationists' defeat.

In January 1995 Garrow proposed that the death-dealing bullets fired in Pensacola and Brookline did not foretell an intensification of the violence against *Roe v. Wade* but were "the death throes of an antiabortion movement in which almost every remaining participant realizes that the war to overturn *Roe v. Wade* has been irretrievably lost." It was lost, he maintained, when the Supreme Court reaffirmed *Roe* with the 1992 decision, *Planned Parenthood v. Casey,* followed by the Freedom of Access to Clinic Entrances Act of 1994, and finally by the courts levying million-dollar penalties against organizations and their leaders for violating women's right to abortion.

"The tragedy of the [clinic] slayings," Garrow concluded, "should not confuse us as to what we are witnessing here: people who kill for 'life' represent the last throes of a struggle in which armed terrorism represents the final fringe."

Time would tell, but the lowering of both the volume and the vehemence of prolife rhetoric in 1995 offered a hopeful sign that people could be both prolife and prochoice and discuss, instead of fight over, legitimate questions about abortion.

Finally two other developments in the mid-1990s promised to change the very nature of abortion and the clash over its use in America.

President Clinton, only two days after taking office, ordered a review of President Bush's ban on the import of a French drug, "mifepristone." Known as RU-486, it was technically an "abortifacent," in this case a pill that in the early stages of pregnancy could medically induce a miscarriage, thereby an abortion. It was patented, manufactured, and sold in France by Roussel-Uclaf, a company that also marketed it in Great Britain, Sweden, and China. However, Roussel-Uclaf had avoided marketing RU-486 in the United States for fear that antiabortion groups would organize boycotts against the firm's other products sold in America. Nevertheless, in 1994 Donna Shalala, President Clinton's secretary of health and human services, announced that Roussel-Uclaf was donating the U.S. patent rights to RU-486 to the Population Council, a nonprofit contraceptive research group. The council agreed to conduct clinical trials of RU-486 and find a U.S. manufacturer that would then apply to the Federal Food and Drug Administration (FDA) for testing and final approval.

This meant it could take several years before American women could use RU-486, which offered many advantages over the procedure approved in the United States. While an American abortion required surgery performed by a qualified gynecologist in a a clinic or hospital, the French version amounted to using a drug prescribed by and administered by almost any physician in the privacy of his or her office. When carried out within forty-nine days of a pregnant woman's last menstrual period, RU-486 had proven nearly 100 percent effective. In America the medical procedure would not only make abortion far more available geographically, it would also avoid the trauma of women having to suffer antiabortion protestors.

The Population Council's clinical trials of RU-486 at cooperating clinics were barely under way in the fall of 1994 when in a surprising development the media reported a most unusual trial of another way to perform medical abortions.

It had begun when an advertisement appeared in the *New York Times* with the headline NONSURGICAL TERMINATION OF PREGNANCY. The copy offered "a new, safe and effective approach to the termination of early pregnancy utilizing FDA-approved medications." Women responding to the ad went to the office of a Park Avenue gynecologist, Dr. Richard Hausknecht, who was associated with the Mount Sinai School of Medicine. If the women agreed to his procedure, and a five-hundred-dollar fee, they received a medical abortion comparable to the French version. By the fall of 1994 Dr. Hausknecht had successfully performed 121 medical abortions, while only 5 others had failed and had to be completed surgically.

In October the doctor revealed what he was doing, not through medical journals, but through a press conference. He had, as advertised, used two FDA-approved medications to perform abortions for patients less than eight weeks pregnant. One of the drugs had been prescribed to treat cancer, arthritis, and "ectopic pregnancies" (severely abnormal ones that the drug would terminate). The second drug, administered four days later, was one used to hasten labor in the birth process. Dr. Hausknecht reported that patients who had previously experienced surgical abortions found his treatment better. One of these women said: "I had some minor discomfort after the injection and then after the pills were inserted I had uterine cramps and bleeding similar to a bad menstrual period. It was more comfortable and less painful than a surgical abortion, and it seemed safer."

Some researchers were highly critical of how Dr. Hausknecht had conducted the trials of his new procedure, but others recognized the importance of what the New York doctor had accomplished and joined him to conduct more conventional, scientifically acceptable trials of his two-drug treatment.

At the end of August 1995 the prestigious *New England Journal of Medicine* published a report by Dr. Hausknecht explaining how he and the other researchers had confirmed the validity of his technique with hundreds of successful abortions. The doctors were also developing procedures and patient counseling methods that would allow any licensed physician to supervise medical abortions with two inexpensive medications (costing around ten dollars for both). It was now clear that the United States had a simple, effective, widely available, much more private way of carrying out what *Roe v. Wade* had guaranteed American women.

This was emphasized in a speech by the president of Planned Parenthood of New York City, Alexander Sanger (grandson of Margaret Sanger). Doctors in the future, he said, could offer "medical abortions in the privacy of their offices in small towns and urban centers throughout the country," and he stressed that this could happen without women being harassed and fearing violence, because the antiabortion movement couldn't picket every medical practitioner in the country.

In privacy, without fear! The medical profession, after nearly a quarter century of trauma over surgical abortions, was complementing the "essential holding" of *Roe v. Wade*: that a woman's, and her doctor's, right to terminate her pregnancy in the early stages is a private matter protected by the Constitution. That is what the 1973 decision was about, not to promote abortions, but to protect the personal privacy of those who chose to have abortions and of the doctors providing them. Not only was the medical profession, along with their patients, affected by endless protests against *Roe,* so were the justices of the Supreme Court. They wavered, and *Roe v. Wade* remained for years in danger of being overruled—until 1992 when a majority of the Court reaffirmed the essential holding of *Roe* in deciding *Planned Parenthood of Southeastern Pennsylvania v. Casey.* With this decision the High Court finally stood firm on its nineteen-year-old abortion decision. And that—not changes in abortion procedures—was the most important change that would affect the future of abortion in America. The decision strengthened the rule of law protecting a woman's right to privacy in regard to abortion. And, in our democracy, the rule of law, well defined and firmly held by the highest court in the land, eventually wins the respect of the people.

Bibliography

Barnum, Phineas Taylor. *Struggles and Triumphs, or, Forty Years' Recollections of P. T. Barnum.* New York: American News Co., 1871.

Brooks, Carol F. "The Early History of the Anti-Contraception Laws in Massachusetts and Connecticut." *American Quarterly* 18 (Spring 1966): 3–23.

Broun, Heywood C., and Margaret Leech. *Anthony Comstock, Roundsman of the Lord.* New York: A. and C. Boni, 1927.

Comstock, Anthony. *Frauds Exposed; or, How the People Are Deceived and Robbed and Youth Corrupted.* New York: J. H. Brown, 1880.

Facts in Brief: Abortion in the United States. New York: Alan Guttmacher Institute, 1995.

Faux, Marian. *Roe v. Wade: The Untold Story of the Landmark Supreme Court Decision That Made Abortion Legal.* New York: Macmillan, 1988.

Garrow, David J. "A Deadly, Dying Fringe." *New York Times,* 6 January 1995, OP-ED page.

———. "Justice Souter Emerges." *New York Times Magazine,* 25 September 1994, pp. 36–67.

———. *Liberty and Sexuality: The Right to Privacy and the Making of Roe v. Wade.* New York: Macmillan, 1994.

Greenhouse, Linda. "How a Ruling on Abortion Took On a Life of Its Own." *New York Times,* 10 April 1994, section 4, p. 3.

Harrell, Mary Ann, and Stuart E. Jones. *Equal Justice Under Law: The Supreme Court in American Life.* Washington: Foundation of the Federal Bar Association, 1965.

Irons, Peter, and Stephanie Guitton, eds. *May It Please the Court.* New York: New Press, 1993.

McCorvey, Norma, with Andy Meisler. *I Am Roe: My Life, Roe v. Wade, and Freedom of Choice.* New York: HarperCollins, 1994.

McKenna, George. "On Abortion: A Lincolnian Position." *The Atlantic Monthly* (September 1995): 51–68.

Newman, Roger K. *Hugo Black: A Biography.* New York: Random House, 1994.

Sanger, Margaret. *My Fight for Birth Control.* New York: Farrar & Rinehart, 1931.

Schwartz, Bernard. *A History of the Supreme Court.* New York: Oxford University Press, 1993.

Seventy-five Years of Family Planning in America; A Chronology of Major Events (booklet). New York: Planned Parenthood Federation of America, 1991.

Topalain, Elyse. *Margaret Sanger.* New York: Franklin Watts, 1984.

Tribe, Laurence H. *Abortion: The Clash of Absolutes.* New York: Norton, 1992.

Weddington, Sarah. *A Question of Choice.* New York: Grosset/Putnam, 1992.

Werner, Morris R. *Barnum.* New York: Harcourt, Brace, 1923.

Glossaries

Legal

Affirm—to uphold the judgment of a lower court, thereby declaring it valid and right, and that it must stand as rendered.

Amicus curiae—"a friend of the court"; a person not party to a case who gives his or her views on the case to a court, either by volunteering or accepting the court's invitation to do so.

Appeal—to take the decision of a court to a higher court to be reviewed and upheld or reversed.

Appellant—the party that appeals a lower-court decision to a higher court (also referred to as a petitioner).

Appellate court—a court having the right to act on appeals from lower courts, but which does not hold trials.

Appellee—one who has an interest in upholding a lower court's decision and responds when the decision is appealed to a higher court (also referred to as a respondent).

Brief—a document prepared by a lawyer to serve as the basis for an argument in court, setting out the facts of and legal arguments in support of the lawyer's case.

Case law—laws that develop from previously decided court cases and are distinct from statutes passed by legislatures.

Class action—a lawsuit brought by a person or group of persons in behalf of all persons similarly situated.

Common law—collections of principles and rules of action deriving their authority from long-standing usage or from courts recognizing and enforcing them.

Concurring opinion—one written by a justice who agrees with the outcome of a decision but may have his or her own reasons for the decision.

Dissenting opinion—one written by a justice expressing disagreement with the outcome of a decision and with the court's treatment of the parties involved. Because Supreme Court cases are decided by majority rule, dissents have no legal force; however, they are important features of decisions, and a dissent may subsequently become more important than the decision itself.

Injunction—a court order prohibiting the person to whom it is applied from performing a particular act.

Judicial—pertains to courts of law and the administration of justice.

Justice—the title given judges, particularly of state supreme courts and the Supreme Court of the United States.

Landmark decision—a Supreme Court decision that fundamentally alters the relationships of Americans to their institutions and to one another.

Moot case or question—one that is, or has become, immaterial because there is no longer any disagreement between the parties involved.

Precedent—a legal decision or procedure which may serve as an authoritative rule or pattern in similar cases in the future.

Stare decisis—"let the decision stand." Thus it refers to the principle of adherence to settled cases and accepting them as authoritative in similar subsequent cases.

Statute—a written law enacted by a legislature.

Supreme Court of the United States—the nation's highest court, composed of the chief justice of the United States and eight associate justices. They are nominated by the president, and their final appointments must be approved by the U.S. Senate.

United States Courts of Appeals—they hear appeals from the U.S. District Courts, and their decisions may be reviewed by the U.S. Supreme Court, but most are final and are not taken by the Supreme Court. The Courts of Appeals cover judicial areas, called circuits, and at the time *Roe v. Wade* was considered there were eleven circuits in the nation.

United States District Courts—the trial courts for federal (as opposed to state) cases. Each state has one or more federal districts, and each district has a district court.

United States Reports—the official printed record of cases heard and decided by the U.S. Supreme Court.

v.—versus or against.

Watershed decision—a Supreme Court decision, as defined by Oliver Wendell Holmes, that "exercise(s) a kind of hydraulic pressure which makes what previously was clear seem doubtful, and before which even well-settled principles of law will bend."

Medical

Abortifacient—anything ingested to induce an abortion.

Abortion—ends pregnancy before birth takes place. An abortion may be performed surgically, induced medically, or occur spontaneously (as a miscarriage, for example).

Abortionist—correctly defines a person who performs illegal abortions, but often incorrectly used as a disparaging term for a person performing a legal abortion.

Birth control—planning to determine family size.

Conception—the beginning of pregnancy.

Contraception—the prevention of conception by various techniques or devices.

Diaphragm—a cup-shaped rubber device inserted into a woman's vagina before sexual intercourse to prevent the male sperm from reaching and fertilizing the female ovum.

Embryo and pre-embryo—the pre-embryo is a ball of cells that develops from fertilization of the ovum. In about nine days it attaches to the lining of the uterus and becomes an embryo that shares the woman's blood supply and, after eight weeks, becomes a fetus.

Fertilization—the joining of the male sperm with the egg in the sexual reproductive process.

Fetus—the organism that develops from the embryo after eight weeks of pregnancy and is nourished through the placenta.

Ovum—the female reproductive cell—the egg.

Placenta—the organism that develops from the fetus and passes nourishment from the woman to her fetus.

Trimester—one of the three-month periods (first, second, and third trimesters) during the nine months of pregnancy.

Appendix A

Justices who served on the Supreme Court of the United States between 1965 and 1993, and the full or partially filled term of each:

Hugo Lafayette Black	1937–1971
William Orville Douglas	1939–1975
Tom Campbell Clark	1949–1967
Earl Warren (chief)	1953–1969
John Marshall Harlan	1955–1971
William Joseph Brennan, Jr.	1956–1990
Potter Stewart	1958–1981
Byron Raymond White	1962–1993
Arthur Joseph Goldberg III	1962–1965
Thurgood Marshall	1967–1991
Warren Earl Burger (chief)	1969–1986
Harry Andrew Blackmun	1970–1994
Lewis Franklin Powell, Jr.	1971–1987
William Hubbs Rehnquist (chief)	1971–
John Paul Stevens	1975–
Sandra Day O'Connor	1981–
Antonin Scalia	1986–
Anthony McLeod Kennedy	1988–
David H. Souter	1990–
Clarence Thomas	1991–
Ruth Bader Ginsburg	1993–

How they participated in four leading right-to-privacy and right-to-abortion cases: *Griswold v. Connecticut, Roe v. Wade, Webster v. Reproductive Health Services,* and *Planned Parenthood v. Casey*:

Griswold	Black, Brennan, Clark, Douglas, Goldberg, Harlan, Stewart, Warren, and White.
Roe	Blackmun, Brennan, Burger, Douglas, Marshall, Powell, Rehnquist, Stewart, and White.

Webster	Blackmun, Brennan, Kennedy, Marshall, O'Connor, Rehnquist, Scalia, Stevens, and White.
Planned Parenthood	Blackmun, Kennedy, O'Connor, Rehnquist, Scalia, Souter, Stevens, Thomas, and White.

Appendix B

Amendments to the Constitution of the United States
that played roles in
Griswold v. Connecticut and *Roe v. Wade*:

FIRST

Congress shall make no law respecting an establishment of religion, or prohibiting the free exercise thereof; or abridging the freedom of speech, or the press; or the right of the people peaceably to assemble, and to petition the Government for a redress of grievances.

FOURTH

The right of the people to be secure in their persons, houses, papers and effects, against unreasonable searches and seizures, shall not be violated, and no warrants shall issue, but upon probable cause, supported by oath or affirmation, and particularly describing the place to be searched, and the persons or things to be seized.

NINTH

The enumeration in the Constitution, of certain rights, shall not be construed to deny or disparage others retained by the people.

FOURTEENTH (SECTION 1)

All persons born or naturalized in the United States and subject to the jurisdiction thereof, are citizens of the United States and of the State wherein they reside. No state shall make or enforce any law which shall abridge the privileges and immunities of citizens of the United States; nor shall any State deprive any person of life, liberty, or property, without the due process of law; nor deny to any person within its jurisdiction the equal protection of the laws.

Index